MOTHERLESS CHILD

Motherless Child

V.M. Burns

CAMEL
PRESS
SEATTLE, WA

CAMEL
PRESS

Camel Press
6524 NE 181st St
Suite 2
Kenmore, WA 98028

For more information go to: www.camelpress.com or
www.vmburns.com

This is a work of fiction. Names, characters, places, brands, media,
and incidents are the product of the author's imagination or are used
fictitiously.

Motherless Child
2017 © by V.M. Burns

ISBN: 978-1-603816-91-5 (trade paper)
ISBN: 978-1-603816-92-2 (ebook)

This book is dedicated to my mom, Elvira Burns and my aunt, Henrietta Thomas.

Acknowledgements

Thanks to Jennifer McCord at Camel Press and Dawn Dowdle at Blue Ridge Literary Agency for helping to make this series a reality.

Special thanks to my Seton Hill University tribe, my Cozy Mystery Crew, Crime Writers of Color and especially to my unicorns (Kellye, Alexia, Abby, et. al). Thank you to my work family, Barnyardians (Tim, Lindsey, Jill and Chuck), our fearless leader (Sandy), my fantastic team (Derrick, Eric, Jennifer, Jonathan, Amber and Robin) and to the team that will always be my team whether you report to me or not (Jamie, Grace, Deborah and Tena).

I don't think I could have gotten this book completed without my family who have had to listen to me gripe, complain, read and review. Thanks to Jackie, Christopher, Carson and Crosby Rucker; Jillian, Drew and Marcella Merkel and to my dad, Benjamin Burns for all of the support and love. I have been blessed with friends who are like family. Thanks to Shelitha Mckee and Sophia Muckerson for all of the support, encouragement and the occasional slap of reality.

Sometimes I feel like a motherless child

Sometimes I feel like a motherless child

Sometimes I feel like a motherless child

A long ways from home

A long ways from home

True believer

A long ways from home

Along ways from home

CHAPTER 1

I came really close to not answering the phone. It was a perfect day in northwest Indiana and I had a feeling in the pit of my stomach that a telephone call on a perfect day would ruin it. Harley, my partner, told me not to answer. But I didn't listen. What constituted a perfect day? For me it was a Saturday in mid-August when the leaves started to change color, the weather had cooled down, the days were shorter, and football season started.

This was the first game of the season and after two years of torture under a coach, who knew about as much about play selection as my grandmother, Mary and Joseph Catholic University in St. Joseph, Indiana, or MAC-U as the locals called it, had finally seen fit to hire a new head coach. Thankfully, we still had some talented players left. And I, recently employed by MAC-U to teach first year law students about law enforcement, was enjoying the perk of half-priced tickets to the MAC-U Raiders' game for the first time ever. Granted, my seats were not even remotely close to the 50-yard line, but thankfully, the stadium is small enough that almost every seat still commanded a great view of the action.

It was half-time and the score was tied. It just didn't get much better. That's when my cell phone rang and put an end to my perfect day.

"Don't answer it," Harley said.

Harley Wickfield IV was my partner and the proud recipient of the second ticket faculty members were allowed to purchase. We were alike in a lot of ways. We were both over six feet tall, slender. At thirty-three I was older, by about seven years, but we had similar personalities. The obvious difference between us was I'm an African American Yankee, born and raised in St.

Joseph, Indiana; while Harley is a southerner from an affluent family. In spite of the obvious, we were more alike in the ways that matter.

I considered not answering for a split second, but one glance at the number showed the call to be from someone I wanted to impress. Reason should have told me Paris wouldn't have called during the game just to chat. But reason had very little to do with matters of the heart; I didn't listen and picked up.

"Score is tied at half-time. You should have come—" was as far as I got.

"You need to get over here right now. There's been a murder."

As a policeman, I'm accustomed to getting calls about murder. However, these usually come from the precinct and not from my girlfriend.

"Who's been killed? Are you ok? Where are you?" I was firing questions faster than she could answer, but a knot had just developed in the pit of my stomach and I was sure it wasn't the hot dogs, nachos, peanuts, or beer I'd already eaten.

"I'm fine. I'm at the American Legion on South Main Street. Can you come? Please?"

Paris Williams was a smart woman and doesn't scare easily. But she was scared.

"I'll be right there. Did anyone call the police?"

She laughed and then added, "I thought that's what I was doing."

CHAPTER 2

MAC-U's stadium was not very far from the American Legion. It took longer for us to get to our car from the stands than it did to drive over.

We took advantage of the short drive to alert the precinct to the murder as we wove between the RVs and trailers tailgating in the parking lot. Even though it was technically my day off, I would most likely have been pulled to work on the case anyway. Everyone was on call during home football weekends. The university paid double for increased security and traffic patrol for home football weekends, and most officers looked forward to the extra pay and volunteered to work. The really lucky ones got to patrol inside the stadium and watched the game. But it still hurt to leave that game.

The roar of the crowd told us the Raiders had scored before the announcer on the radio did. We listened to the game in the car as we drove to the American Legion. One look from Harley spoke volumes. Thankfully, he didn't say anything and we drove in silence.

The American Legion was a rectangular building on the corner of South Main and 20th Streets in St. Joseph, Indiana. It was a long low building that resembled an airplane hangar. There was guest parking on the side and in the back. As we pulled up to the building there was a crowd of people standing around in what my godmother, Mama B, would call their 'Sunday going to meeting clothes.'

In a bright green T-shirt and jeans, I didn't exactly look the part of a competent law enforcement professional, but I put my shield on to lend an air of authority and headed inside.

Inside, it was clear the wedding which was normally the start of a new life, had been interrupted and people were standing or sitting around trying to decide how to react. The manager came up and introduced himself to us and then led us to the back of the building. We had to walk through the kitchen to get to a small room, at the back of the kitchen.

Half of the kitchen staff stood around whispering. The other half smoked outside. The door at the back of the kitchen was closed and that's where I found Paris, standing guard.

We had only been dating for three months, but I still felt my pulse race a bit when I saw her. Paris was tall, which worked considering I was six foot three. She had a medium build with dark skin as smooth as chocolate milk and light grey eyes with golden flecks that sparkled when she smiled. She was curvy and as a stylist and salon owner, she had a certain flair that showcased her attributes to the best of their ability.

I felt my lips twitch into a smile when I saw her, but quickly remembered why we were here. "What happened?" I asked.

Paris opened the door and stepped back to allow us to enter. "I don't know. I was in the main part of the building watching the festivities when I heard someone scream. I came with everyone else back here and saw him." She inclined her head toward the body on the ground.

Harley went over and checked for a pulse, but given the huge knife sticking out of his chest, neither one of us expected to find one.

"Who found him?" I looked around.

That's when the manager pointed to a woman who was shaking and crying in a corner by the sink.

"Who is he?" I directed the question at Paris, but pointed to the corpse.

"The Father of the Bride."

CHAPTER 3

The waitress who found the body claimed she had a headache and went to the back room to lie down for a few minutes. She saw the dead man and screamed. She didn't know him or any of the family. She hadn't seen anything, nor had she touched anything. Her story was pretty simple and the interview took less than twenty minutes.

Some of the guests hadn't been able to hear her screams over the music, dancing, and overall mirth and merriment. Apparently, the word spread mostly by word of mouth. Like Lemmings, others followed the group they saw running to the back. At some point, the decision was made that it would be in poor taste to continue partying while the bride's father lay dead in the back room. That's when the music halted, and the drinking intensified. I noticed several of the groomsmen were shirtless and plastered.

"What happened to their shirts?" I asked Paris.

"Don't ask. This is like a bad frat party. The drinking started from the moment the wedding was over and hasn't stopped." Paris sounded disgusted. "There were a couple of…accidents."

I managed to grab Paris and guide her to a quiet corner where I could make sure she was really okay and where we could talk privately.

"Do you know these people? I thought you said you were working today?" If I sounded a little miffed, it was due entirely to concern for her safety rather than missing the football game, but I'm not sure she knew that.

"I *am* working," She huffed. "I was hired to do the hair and makeup for the bride and the bridal party. In fact, I have been working since almost 7:00 o'clock this morning, so don't yell at me Robert James Franklin Jr." If the fact she used my full name, rather than RJ, wasn't a clue she was mad, the look in her eyes, the roll of her neck and the hand on her hip certainly made it quite clear that she was more than a little upset.

"I'm sorry. I wasn't yelling." I tried to placate, but one look and I knew she was on the edge.

"Ok. I was yelling, but I'm sorry, really. But I don't like the idea of you anywhere near some knife wielding maniac. That man was murdered and whoever did it could have...It might have been you."

I must have looked pretty pathetic because she managed a short laugh and then walked into my arms.

"Just give me a hug before I break down and cry."

I complied and after a few moments, we both felt better.

She pulled away and breathed a heavy sigh before saying, "I'm okay now. What do you want to know?"

"Who is he?"

"His name is John Paul Rollins."

"Rollins? *The* John Paul Rollins of Rollins Trucking, Rollins Freight, and Rollins Rentals?"

"Yes. And it's his daughter that got married today. Technically, she's his niece."

I must have looked confused, because she stopped, shrugged and shook her head, "It's complicated."

"I guess so. How can she be his daughter *and* his niece?"

"Biologically, she's his niece, his brother's child. However, when she was a baby her parents were killed in a car accident, and he adopted her and raised her as his daughter."

I nodded. "Sounds reasonable. So, what happened?"

"I honestly don't know. I've only met them a couple of times. Once when they came in for a consultation and then again for a dry run a couple of weeks ago."

"Dry run?"

She nodded. "Once she got her veil, I did her hair and makeup so she could choose the look that she wanted and to make sure it was exactly how she wanted to look. That's common with weddings."

"Was Mr. Rollins there?"

"Only for the first session; he interviewed me and looked through my portfolio. Of course, I saw him this morning at the church and then later here."

"If you did the hair and makeup this morning, then why are you here at the reception?"

"Because she wanted me to refresh her makeup for the pictures." She shrugged. "They paid extra for it. I was finished and was taking my bags out to my car. I parked in front to make things easier. That's when I heard the screams."

"Did you see or hear anything that will help? Was there a fight? Did anyone threaten him?"

She was shaking her head before I finished. "Not that I saw. I didn't really know any of these people personally, so I don't know how they behave normally. Weddings are always a little tense." She thought for a moment. "He liked to give orders. And his daughter liked disobeying them. They seemed a bit odd, I don't know..." She shrugged and shook her head again.

"What. Anything, what is it?"

She paused for a while then sighed. "It's just that he was a strange man. He was rich, but cheap. I mean, look at this place." She waved her hand around the American Legion Hall. "It's not that the building isn't nice, but he could certainly afford to do a lot better for his only child and heir to his wealth." She shook her head.

"Anything else?"

She folded her arms across her chest. "He tried to stiff me on my fee after we had agreed to a price." She put her hand on her hip in a way that told me Mr. Rollins had met his match in Paris Williams. "But, I was firm." She shook her head.

"He was a man who was used to getting his own way."

I expected a snide remark, but to her credit, none came.

"I need to go and talk to the daughter. I'm assuming she's the one in the white dress." I motioned to a group of people outside who had come into the kitchen and were huddled near the back door.

Paris smiled as she shook her head. "You'd be wrong. That's the Maid of Honor. The Bride is the one in red." She inclined her head towards a slightly plump woman in a long, formal evening gown of scarlet red. Her hair was jet black as were her fingernails and lipstick. In contrast, her skin looked extremely white.

I cocked an eyebrow and tilted my head to the side allowing my body language to ask the question *what did you do to her?*

Paris smiled and shrugged her shoulders, "I do what the client asks."

Apparently what this client asked for was a gothic look. I should have known when I saw the three-tiered wedding cake in the main room. The cake was white with red roses around each tier - nothing unusual there. The unusual thing was the large black spider and spider web that had been added to the cake.

The manager loaned me his office for interviews. The office was a small room located just up a set of rickety stairs off the back of the kitchen. I ushered the bride and groom there and closed the door. Although the walls didn't go all the way to the ceiling, it did give a sense of privacy. The space was barely large enough for a desk, file cabinet and chair. With Harley and I and the bride and groom, I was grateful that the walls didn't go to the ceiling. I think I would have been claustrophobic if it did.

Regardless of my personal preferences, I knew this young woman had just lost her father, so I started by expressing sympathy. "Miss Rollins I'm very sorry for your loss—"

"Mrs. Stevens. Mrs. Samantha Stevens. Isn't that cool? I mean, as soon as I heard Todd's last name, I knew we were destined to be together?"

I must have looked as lost as I felt, because she prattled on at a quick pace, "You know, Samantha Stevens? Bewitched? I *loved* that show. She was so cool. I used to dream of being a witch when I was a little girl. Then, I could twitch my nose and make everything the way I wanted." She tried a nose twitch but failed. "But, I would have liked to have been more like Serena then Samantha. Samantha was always so good, and Serena liked to have fun. But they were both played by the same woman, so that's okay." She took a breath, and smiled at her husband, who kissed her.

Todd smiled, squeezed her shoulder and then smiled again.

Even if I couldn't tell by the blood shot eyes, slurred speech and disheveled appearance, the smell would have let me know without a doubt that the groom was as drunk as a skunk. He absolutely reeked of alcohol. I was amazed he was able to make it up the stairs to the office.

I've been a cop for more than a decade, and I'd seen people handle grief a lot of different ways, but Samantha Stevens was a first for me. "Mrs. Stevens when was the last time you saw your father alive?"

"I don't know. I think it was right after we started shots."

Harley almost fell off his perch. "Excuse me?" Up till then, he had been so quiet, perched on a corner of the desk that I had just about forgotten he was there.

He looked puzzled and repeated himself. "Did you say shots? You mean photo shots of the wedding?"

Both the bride and groom laughed so hard I thought they would fall off their chairs.

Mrs. Stevens regained her composure first. Perhaps because she was slightly less plastered than her husband. "No, *Shots*. You know." With one motion she tossed her head back and used her arm to indicate that the shots they were doing had nothing to do with cameras and everything to do with the liquor which seemed to have been flowing very freely all afternoon.

After they finished giggling, I tried again, "Mrs. Stevens, what time was that?"

More giggling, "I guess it must have been around three-thirty or so. We had just finished eating, so I think that's about right."

"And what was your father doing when you started doing shots?" I didn't really try to keep the contempt out of my voice. This pampered brat was sitting here giggling at me while the man who raised her was lying dead downstairs.

"Oh, he was doing shots too. There were few things that JP Rollins liked more than his booze." Mrs. Stevens was certainly not the picture of mourning in her red dress. Her attitude was consistent.

"He was doing Jager Shots at the bar before we had even been served our meal." Mr. Todd Stevens managed to squeak out before he belched and then burst into another round of laughter.

I've never been a big drinker. But I did spend four years at college where I learned what a Jager shot included. Not exactly, what I would imagine the father of the bride would be doing at his daughter's wedding.

"When did your father go to the back room?" Harley tried again.

"I don't know. I wasn't really paying him a lot of attention. It *IS* my wedding day, after all." Mrs. Stevens made a gesture indicating her red dress and veil, which was slightly askew and tried, unsuccessfully to sit straighter.

"Yes. We can see that. Congratulations. But, Mrs. Stevens, someone killed your father in the middle of your wedding reception. Do you know anyone who would want to do that?" I leaned in as I stared from one of them to the other, hopefully instilling the seriousness of the situation on them. I failed.

Mrs. Stevens looked me dead in the eye, leaned close and said "Hell officer, just about everyone who ever met JP hated his guts. You'd have an easier time finding someone who didn't want him dead."

CHAPTER 4

Harley's look of disbelief was almost comical. I probably would have laughed too if I weren't so incredibly frustrated by the newlyweds who were laughing so hard, tears were streaming down their faces. Those were the only tears I'd seen from the daughter of JP Rollins or her husband.

I'd decided to try a different approach. "Perhaps you can tell me why so many people hated your father?"

"Well, first off he wasn't really my father. He was my uncle." Holding up her hand, she ticked off each item. "He was demanding. Selfish. Arrogant and evil." Finished counting, she added, "everything had to be his way or no way. He held the purse strings and he never let you forget it. He wanted to control everyone." Mrs. Stevens eyes flashed as she spoke; but at least she wasn't laughing.

"Did he try to control you?" I asked.

"Only my entire life. He wanted to tell me where to live and where to go and what to wear." She leaned closer. "You know he even tried to pick my wedding dress. But I fooled him. I let him pick the dress alright but when it came, I took it and I dyed it red." She preened.

"I see and did that anger your father...um I mean Mr. Rollins?"

"Oh yeah, you should have seen his face this morning. I thought he was going to explode right there in the church in front of everyone. I could barely keep from laughing as I was walking down the aisle." She didn't try to keep from laughing now.

I rubbed my forehead and slid a glance at Harley, who was taking notes in the corner. He was new to homicide and was getting good exposure with this case.

"How did Mr. Rollins take it? I'm sure he didn't just roll over and say nothing to you after that?"

"Oh, he tried to yell at me at the church. But it was too late then. I thought he would refuse to walk me down the aisle." She frowned in disappointment. "But no such luck. I guess he figured that would make me happy so he wasn't about to give in and let me have the wedding I wanted."

"Didn't his attempts to control you make you mad?" Harley asked quietly from the corner.

"It used to, when I was younger. Now, I know how to get back at him, so it wasn't so bad anymore." She said smugly.

"How did you get back at him?" I asked softly.

But the light bulb finally went on and her eyes flashed, "I didn't kill him if that's what you're thinking."

"Who did?" I asked as politely as I could given the circumstances.

"I have no idea. And, I wouldn't tell you even if I did."

"Why not? Don't you want to see justice done to the man or woman who killed your uncle…ah, father?"

"Justice? Ha! JP Rollins wouldn't know the meaning of the word." She stood up.

"Come on Todd, let's get out of here. We've got a plane to catch."

"Excuse me?" I asked.

"A plane. We've got airline tickets. It's my honeymoon you know."

Harley's mouth was hanging open. But he managed to sputter, "Surely you don't plan to go on your honeymoon now. I mean, you'll need to see to the burial of your father ah… I mean your uncle."

"You may not have cared for your uncle, but he's dead," I added.

She stared at me as though I was an alien. "I have non-refundable airline tickets to Florida and reservations to Disney World. There's no way I'm missing my honeymoon. He's dead. He'll keep." And with that, Mrs. Stevens turned, but must have done it too quickly. She wobbled, reeled, and then righted herself. Apparently the motion of turning too rapidly combined with the alcohol did not sit very well with Mrs. Stevens. She looked green, clutched her hand to her mouth, wrenched the door open and ran down the stairs toward the restroom.

Looking down the stairs, I saw her puking in a large garbage can in the kitchen.

Mr. Todd Stevens needed more help rising from his chair. Harley reached out a hand and pulled him up. He stumbled to his feet. Harley propped him against the desk and then looked the question that we were both wondering. How were we going to get him down the stairs?

I wasn't willing to risk his making it to the trash can as quickly as his wife. I opened the door and called to one of the uniformed policeman downstairs to assist in getting him down. This was certainly a strange family.

By the time the coroner had finished and removed the body, Harley and I had taken statements from the kitchen staff, the bridal party and any of the guests who were sober enough to talk coherently. We got names, addresses, and telephone numbers from everyone and waited until the crime scene crew finished going over the place. About three hours after I arrived, I was finally back in my car and heading home.

Paris had gone home a couple of hours earlier. Harley had ridden to the football game with me, so his car was still at my house. In the car, we learned that the MAC-U Raiders had won the game handily by a score of 42 – 21. Harley's look said it all. I shouldn't have answered the phone, but it was too late now. We were on the case and the next few days would be hectic trying to figure out which one of those people had driven a knife through the heart of JP Rollins.

CHAPTER 5

A year ago, I was in a car accident. The accident hadn't been my fault, but it had resulted in fatalities, including a small child. I've seen a lot of horrible things in my time, but nothing shook me as much as that little kid's death. The nightmares no longer came every night, but they were still frequent visitors which invaded my sleep. Early the next morning I drug myself out of bed, showered, dressed and drove to church for the early service. I was a mite late, but I was there nonetheless. Arriving only thirty minutes late for the eight am service is a feat to be applauded. Before I met Paris Williams, I would not have even contemplated attending the early service. But, three months ago that all changed. Paris is actively involved with the choirs, and often sings at eight o'clock. We met when I was investigating the death of our last choir director and I was pretty well a goner from the first moment I laid eyes on her. Fortunately for me the feeling appeared to be mutual.

First Baptist Church, or FBC as the members and most of the community called it, had been around for well over seventy years. The building was a classic brick structure with stained glass windows and lots of woodwork. The pews, the walls, the pulpit and the altar were a vision of mid-century craftsmanship and a pain to keep dusted and clean.

The usher recognized me and led me to the pew where my godmother, Mama B, was already seated. One glance at me and she moved the suitcase she called a pocket book, and slid down to allow me to sit on the end. I was tall and she knew I liked stretching my legs in the aisle.

I kissed Mama B on the cheek and took a long look at the large hat she wore.

Mama B was from that older generation of church matrons who never dreamt of arriving in church without wearing her best Sunday attire, which always included a hat of some type. Today, she was wearing a gray hat that fit snugly around her head but had the most enormous bow I'd ever seen, which was outlined in rhinestones. I looked behind me; certain no one sitting anywhere behind her would be able to see around that massive bow. I received a swipe with her bible. Mama B had an uncanny knack of reading my mind.

"You're late. Now sit up and pay attention." Mama B scolded me just as she did when I was five-years-old. Then she smiled and handed me a peppermint.

Today was the third Sunday in the month which meant youth day at FBC. Each Sunday of the month meant something different; a different choir sang, or different rituals were observed. The first Sunday all of the choirs sang, communion was served and that's the Sunday when people were baptized. The older women typically wore white and there was a general air of pomp and formality. On the second Sunday of the month, the Gospel Chorus and Senior Choir sang. Paris sang with the Gospel Chorus. It consisted of adults and the music was generally more upbeat and contemporary. On the Third Sunday the young adult choir and children sang. The fourth Sunday was the inspirational choir which consisted of older women and men who sang spirituals and anthems. And on those rare months with five Sundays, the male chorus sang.

The young adults and children performed. The junior ushers manned the doors and directed the congregation through the various stages of the service. We even had a young person serve as the church clerk who read the morning announcements.

The children's choir was one of my favorites. This group of enthusiastic kids ranged in ages from five to twelve. In the past, they always wore white blouses and navy blue slacks for the boys and navy skirts for the girls. However, through some active fundraising, they were now sporting stylish new robes which they wore with pride. They were bright purple and golden yellow and were quite a sight to behold. They swayed from side to side and clapped their hands mostly to the beat of the music. They rocked and sang with exuberance and a lack of inhibition that only existed in young children who hadn't yet learned to care what anyone thought about them. They sang a rousing, if not harmonically accurate, rendition of *Yes Jesus Loves Me*, which had the entire church standing, smiling and singing along.

Today, Paris had volunteered to help direct the children's choir. After our last choir director was murdered and discovered to be an adulterous, embezzling, money-laundering thief, the pastor was understandably being a lot more cautious about finding a replacement. Since Paris was on the selection committee that evaluated and interviewed potential candidates, I knew the committee had narrowed their search to three candidates. Starting next month, each candidate would have one week to work with the choir of their choice and select music, rehearse with the choir, and perform on Sunday morning for the congregation. On a personal note, Rev. Hamilton had asked for a thorough background check on each of these candidates, quietly and discreetly. He was a man of God, but was certainly no fool.

I wasn't a fan of the early service, but the one thing I liked best was that it was short, relatively speaking. Sunday school started at nine-thirty, so the early service had to be done before nine-thirty. The eleven o'clock service was generally two hours. The choir sang more songs at the eleven o'clock service and if things ran a little over, no one was pressured to cut it short. Not so with the early service. I considered it a small reward for those diligent enough to get up this early.

By ten o'clock, Paris, Mama B and I were sitting on the front porch at Mama B's house enjoying the basketball game at the recreation center across the alley. These were not your well-mannered, elite athletes who played ball at the Southeast side recreation center. No, these were fierce, die hard ballers. Current and former high school stars, has-beens, wanna-bes, and dreamers hung out and fought for respect on that court almost every day of the week when the weather and daylight permitted.

Mama B lived on the southeast side of town, in a neighborhood that was once home to the middle-class workers of St. Joe. Now the area was considered *the hood*. The buildings were old, derelict and mostly boarded up. The grass was overgrown and the homes that remained were shabby and run down. Mama B lived on an alley across from the recreation center. I used to worry about her safety. But, after close to fifty years in the same location, Mama B was well known and loved by the gangsters and thugs that frequented the area. You were as likely to see a city commissioner sitting on the porch with Mama B as you would see a gang-banger. And Mama B treated all of them the exact same way. Ella Bethany, Mama B to me and my sister, had been my mother's best friend for many years and helped see us through my mom's battle with cancer. Both my mom and dad were gone now and my sister had moved to Houston with her husband and two kids. Now, it was just me and Mama B. She was kind and wise. My partner Harley referred to her as 'The Oracle.' She certainly had a way of reading people that was surprisingly accurate.

She had just finished heating Sunday dinner which we usually ate by noon at the latest. To Mama B, dinner came at noon and supper was served around five. Today she had ham, potatoes and green beans, potato salad, and black-eyed peas. I think I saw a lemon meringue pie in the fridge too. She was an excellent cook and fed anyone who lingered longer than a split second on the porch.

Like clockwork, visitors started arriving after the second service ended. When I saw the first cars arrive, I stood up to take my leave.

"How about a walk around the river?" I asked Paris.

She and Mama B exchanged knowing glances, and they both smiled. I loved my godmother, but I did not want to get trapped listening to the elder members of the congregation as they gossiped and discussed their ailments all afternoon.

Paris rose and went in the house to get her purse.

Mama B smiled as she continued to rock. Not missing a beat, she added "I made you a plate. It's in the fridge."

She never sent me home without a plate. The food was just one of the reasons I enjoyed coming over to see her. She was an excellent cook and the food was definitely a bonus. If the way to a man's heart was through his stomach, Mama B had certainly found mine.

Paris came out, carrying two plates of food. Since she and I started dating about three months ago, Mama B had started sending both of us home with food. Paris claimed she had gained 10 lbs since we started dating. I couldn't see it, but if she'd gained weight, then it was distributed into all of the right places.

We left just as the first car was approaching and waved as we headed toward the river. Walking on the river was a favorite past time for lazy Sunday afternoons. Paris and I walked just about every Sunday since we'd met. As the owner of two successful beauty salons, Paris worked a lot of late hours. As a homicide cop, my schedule was crazy too. But we tried to make time each Sunday to catch up.

We walked hand-in-hand along the river walk, taking in the beauty of the autumn colors, bikers, lovers, and dog walkers meandering around the East Race, and enjoyed the sounds of the St. Joseph River as it lapped against the banks.

"Any progress on the case?"

I work a lot of cases, but I didn't need to ask which case she was referring to. "Not yet. It's too early."

We walked on in a companionable silence but I was curious. "How did you meet JP Rollins?"

"First time I met him was when he walked into my shop and asked me about doing his daughter's hair and makeup for her wedding."

"Is that normal?"

"Yeah, I guess. The best advertisement is word of mouth. I assumed he'd seen my work somewhere, but –"

"But what?"

"It's not unusual for someone to contact me because they've seen my work. What was unusual was that he was the one that contacted me. Usually men don't think about a woman's hair and makeup. Usually it's the bride who comes to me, not the groom, and definite *not* the father of the bride."

I thought about it for a moment. I assumed women put on their own makeup, unless they were celebrities, so I could see why the bride would want to select her own stylist. I suppose that's just an example of how JP Rollins tried to control his daughter. "I take it the Goth look was her idea, not her father's?"

She nodded. "When I did the dry run, I made her up in a classic style that was beautiful and elegant. Yesterday, when I showed up, that's when she pulled the switch."

"I take it JP Rollins wasn't at all happy?"

She smiled at the thought. "That's an understatement. He didn't want to pay me. He tried to say he hadn't hired me to make his daughter look like a freak. But, I wasn't about to put up with being stiffed liked that."

I looked sideways at Paris and noticed the steel in her eyes that I'd seen so often in my sister.

"So, what did you do?"

"I got up in his face and told him that he darned well would be paying me and I whipped out a copy of the contract I'd made him sign and told him that he'd pay me today or he'd pay me later, but one way or another he would pay."

"How did he take that? I got the impression from what I'd heard about him, that JP Rollins liked getting his own way."

"He was ticked off. He stood there fuming and sputtering. But after about ten seconds he burst out laughing. He said he liked a woman with spunk."

I stared at her. "Really?" I tried not to laugh, but I couldn't help myself.

"Yeah, really." She hesitated. "Then he tried to kiss me."

"HE WHAT?" I stopped and looked hard at Paris. "Why didn't you tell me? Did he hurt you?"

"No, he didn't hurt me. I didn't tell you because it wasn't a big deal. He tried, but I was ready for him. I took a self-defense class at the community college a year ago. I brought my size ten pumps down on his foot as hard as I could, and then kneed him in the groin. He dropped like a lead balloon."

The anger I felt two seconds earlier diminished in a flash at the mental image of JP Rollins on his knees. "Then what happened?"

"I told him I wanted my money and he'd better give it to me or I'd tell my boyfriend the cop."

I smiled in spite of myself. Paris, tried to play it cool, attempted to walk away, but I pulled her to me and kissed her.

After a few moments, she pushed away. "Okay officer, that's enough." She smiled. "We'd better keep going before we get arrested for disorderly behavior or something." She smiled again. We continued to walk hand in hand.

I loved Sunday afternoons.

CHAPTER 6

Monday morning, Harley and I sat in the office of our Chief of Police. Chief Mike Barinski, or *Chief Mike* as we all called him, was a large man who looked more like a linebacker for the Indianapolis Colts than a Chief of Police. He had a reputation for being tough but fair. I didn't know anyone on the force who didn't respect him, me included.

Harley and I had found ourselves on high profile cases before. Well, as high profile as it got in a town of only one hundred thousand people. But, JP Rollins was about as close as St. Joseph, Indiana came to royalty. He was a self-made millionaire who owned businesses all over town. The rumors were that if you added all of his businesses, investments, real estate, stocks, and every other pie he had his fingers in all together, JP Rollins was raking in over one million dollars per day. That was a nice little chunk of change and would be bringing a lot of media attention to our department.

"What do you mean his daughter went to Disney World?" Chief Mike looked at me like a dog at a new bowl —one of Mama B's favorite sayings.

"They weren't exactly a tight-knit family." Harley added, although his lips twitched and I knew he was trying his best to hide a smile.

"We didn't have enough to hold her or her husband. Not yet anyway." I added.

"Besides, we got the flight information and hotel information for Disney World." Harley chimed in.

"I've alerted the airports that if either one of them try to leave the state, they will let us know. But, I didn't think you would want to antagonize the only living relation by prohibiting her from going on her honeymoon." I said.

Chief Mike still looked like he couldn't comprehend what we were saying. "But she didn't want to stay and see to her father's burial. You mean she left him there and went to...to Disney World?" Apparently Chief Mike was finding this type of indifference a bit hard to take in.

"Yes Sir. That's what we're saying." Harley confirmed.

Chief Mike continued to look from one of us to the other as if waiting for the punch-line. Eventually, he had to accept that we weren't playing a joke and were indeed stating the truth. He shook his head as though he was trying to clear out the cobwebs. "Wait 'til the press hears about that. Geez! You'd think she could afford to pay to get her dates moved...How do I spin this?" He paced. "Do we tell the media that the daughter was so cold-hearted she abandoned the man who raised and supported her since she was a baby to go to Disney World?" He paced and talked. "While her uncle or father or whatever he was, while his killer ran free, she toddles off to enjoy herself at the *happiest place on earth*." He shook his head. "Does she have any idea how bad that looks?" He stared at us for several moments then continued to pace. He mumbled, "Or, do we hold back and shield her in the event that she is totally innocent and may one day own every newspaper in the county and possibly the banks that hold my mortgage?

"I think we tell the truth as we know it and let the chips fall where they may." I added. "Corny as it sounds; I believe honesty is the best policy. You never have to apologize for the truth."

"Disney World. Of all places. She's going to Disney World. I can just hear the reporters now. 'And where did the richest person in St. Joe go after her father was found murdered?' just like some freakin' Super Bowl commercial." Chief Mike paced faster as he spoke. Unfortunately, his office wasn't much bigger than a handicapped stall in a restaurant bathroom, so he could only take 2-3 steps before he had to turnaround.

I couldn't help thinking about the Energizer Bunny seeing him bluster and huff as he paced.

"Well leaving was her choice. We tried to talk to her, once she sobered up anyway. But, she was determined." I said.

"Short of arresting her as a material witness, what else could we do?" Harley pleaded.

"I can't wait to hear what the Mayor is going to say when he hears this. I've got an appointment with him in thirty minutes."

Now I understood why Chief Mike seemed more anxious than normal. Mayor Longbow always made the chief nervous, even though they had a good relationship, all things considered. I think Chief Mike didn't feel comfortable around politicians. And, Mayor Longbow was definitely a politician. Mama B said when he smiled he looked like he had more teeth than a piano has keys. But, despite that analogy, she liked the mayor. I think she voted for him twice.

Harley and I were, thankfully excluded from this visit to the Mayor's office and left Chief Mike to pace in silence while we went to check the coroner's report and find ourselves a murderer.

The Coroner's report was sitting on our desks by the time we arrived; which just goes to show how important JP Rollins was. The coroner's office was always back logged. But they had obviously put in a lot of overtime and expedited the results.

It didn't come as a surprise that the cause of death was due to the large knife that was sticking out of his chest when we found him. The coroner's report cited murder by a single stab wound to the left chest which perforated the heart. The murderer thoughtfully left the murder weapon behind, although there were no fingerprints to tell us who plunged it into his chest. But sometimes what's missing from the crime scene can be as important as what was there. In this case, there were no fingerprints on the murder weapon which meant the murderer wiped the knife clean. The kitchen staff would have been justified if their fingerprints were found on the murder weapon. The absence of fingerprints might mean that the murderer wasn't someone who would normally handle the cutlery. Or, it could just mean that the murderer watched forensic shows on television and knew enough to wipe the murder weapon clean.

"What do you think?" Harley asked as he read through the report over my shoulder.

"I think I need to talk to the coroner." I got up and headed out of the office.

Harley followed. "Why? What're you looking for?"

Harley was relatively new to homicide, or special crimes. He'd been assigned to me three months ago to help learn the ropes and we'd hit it off immediately, but he wasn't as skilled as I was and still had a lot of questions.

"Just wondering how much force would be needed to plunge the knife in his chest."

The new Coroner's office was in the basement of the annex across the parking lot from our office. The old office was a dank, dark closet in the basement of the station. The new office was a lot lighter although it was still very sterile and cold. It didn't take more than five minutes to make the walk over.

"You want to know if a woman, say…his daughter for instance, could have had enough strength to stab him?" Harley asked as we entered the door and swiped our badges to go to the secure area of the morgue.

He may not have had the years of experience I had, but he was a quick study. "Yep."

CHAPTER 7

The coroner was a short, round man who resembled the classic description of Santa Claus. He was round, jolly, with piercing blue eyes, white beard, and a belly, like a bowl full of jelly. Add a cigar, and a British accent and you've got Percival Cottsworth. We called him 'Sir Percy,' even though he'd never been knighted. He came to the states on an exchange program in college, and never left. He loved the weather in Florida, the casinos in Vegas and the quiet life in Indiana which he said reminded him of home, which was in the Kent countryside. Everyone loved Sir Percy, but today he wasn't as helpful as I would have liked. The knife was exceptionally sharp and wouldn't have required a lot of force. A woman or a man could have done it.

Harley and I had an appointment with JP Rollins' lawyer, Richard Stout, in an hour. Hopefully, there would be something in the will that would indicate who had a financial reason to kill him. In the meantime, we went through the statements taken at the wedding in the hopes someone saw something we could investigate. So far, we knew JP Rollins went to the back room to lie down about an hour before he was found. The kitchen staff was busy preparing and serving the food and wasn't paying attention to the comings and goings. However, there was a second bathroom just outside of the room where JP Rollins was murdered. Apart from the kitchen staff, several people from the wedding party used that rest room. The bride and groom, the best man, father of the bride and the maid of honor all admitted to using the back facilities at one point or another. It would have been very easy to grab a knife on your way to the bath room and to slip into the back room and use it.

We hadn't totally eliminated the kitchen staff, but so far nothing linked any of them to JP Rollins. We were hopeful Rollins attorney would shed some light on the situation for us.

Richard Stout had an office in the old Waterman Building downtown, almost directly across the street from one of Paris' Salons. The Waterman Building was once a grand building with marble floors, and chandeliers and a regal staircase. As a boy, I remembered going into the building once with my mom and being threatened to within an inch of my life if I dared touch anything or embarrassed her in any way. Funny, I don't even remember why we were in the building, but I definitely remembered the threats. Now, the Waterman Building looked old, and smelled musty. What remained of the marble floors was chipped and dingy. The chandeliers looked rusty and dim and the carpets on the stair case looked threadbare and worn. The building was old and sad. The historic preservation society was mounting a drive to save these old buildings, but I questioned if teardown might be a better option in this case.

Stout's office was on the second floor, and after taking a look at the rickety looking elevator, Harley and I decided the stairs would be our best option. There were only two offices on the second floor, so it wasn't hard to find the one we wanted.

Turning left up the stairs, we walked the short distance to the end of the dark hall, and found the glass door that led to the law office of Richard Stout.

From the hall, Stouts office had a small reception area. There were four chairs and a small desk. No one was sitting at the reception desk, but the door behind the reception area was open, so we walked in.

"Mr. Stout?" I said.

JP Rollins attorney, Richard Stout was a gray-haired man most likely in his late fifties or early sixties. He was fit and tanned to an unnatural degree. Shaking our hands, he motioned for us to have a seat. "I've been expecting you. Please, make yourselves comfortable."

Once we were seated, he didn't waste time with formalities.

"You want the particulars about the will." He flipped through a document on his desk. "JP Rollins was a widower and didn't have children of his own. His niece, whom he later adopted, was his sole heir and is beneficiary to his estate."

"How much are we talking about?" I didn't want to beat around the bushes either.

He put on a pair of reading glasses and glanced through the document. "We'll need to have an audit, but I think we're talking somewhere in the neighborhood of 1.2 Billion."

Harley whistled and I tried to imagine our tattooed Goth princess leading a 1.2 billion dollar company. My imagination apparently wasn't that good because try as I might, I couldn't see it.

"You can't be serious? He left that much money to the Goth princess?" I didn't realize I'd said it out loud until I saw Stout's face register the comment. He smiled.

Stout tried to hide his smile, but had to give up. "Well, yes and no. She will inherit. However, JP was no fool. He knew she was ill equipped to run the company. She will inherit the company, but all of the decisions will have to be made by trustees until she reaches the age of thirty."

"Thirty? Isn't that a bit older than usual for an inheritance?" Harley asked.

"Definitely, but well…let's face it gentleman, you've met Samantha. She isn't exactly Oprah Winfrey. I think JP hoped when she got older, she'd have more sense. He thought this was just a phase." Stout waved his arms as if everything in the office was included in the phase.

"So what does this mean?" I was still puzzled.

"It means that for the most part nothing really changes for Samantha. She'll get an allowance to live on. She'll be able to live in the house, drive the car and continue her life just as she has for the past twenty years." He removed his reading glasses. "She will not be able to sell any of the businesses, the property or make any financial decisions without first getting the approval of two out of three of her trustees." Stout leaned back in his chair as he recited the details to us. He stared at us across his desk.

"Who are the trustees?" Harley took out his notebook to jot down names.

"Myself, Frank Logan, VP of Operations for JP Rollins Enterprises, and Mrs. Henrietta Thomas, President of First State Bank."

"Does she know this? Samantha?" I asked.

"I don't think so." Stout shrugged. "She had to know JP well enough to know he wouldn't let her ruin everything he'd built up. She certainly knew JP liked a certain amount of control. But, I don't think she knew the specifics of the will. In fact, I seriously doubt if she did." He leaned forward. "JP just made some of these changes a few days ago."

"Before her marriage?" I asked.

He nodded.

In reflecting on this information, another question came to mind. "What did Mr. Rollins think about her fiancé?"

Here, Stout got up and paced, his first sign of agitation since our arrival. "JP didn't trust him. He thought he was a shiftless, gold digging, dead beat and he didn't care who knew it, including Todd Stevens himself."

"But this didn't deter her?" Harley asked half-heartedly. Having met her, I was sure he already knew the answer to that question before he asked.

"If anything, it fanned the flames even more. JP tried to get them to sign a prenuptial agreement, but they both refused."

"Wow. So, Todd Stevens gets half of everything?" Harley's disbelief was apparent.

"Not exactly. When I said Samantha's life would be basically the same as it was before, I meant it. She will have an allowance to live on, but it's not as much as you would think. He basically provided for her to have a roof over her head, food, clothes and a car. Her husband is not entitled to anything because in the eyes of the law, the estate isn't hers; not yet anyway. If they marry and stay married until she reaches the age of thirty, then he could get half. However, if they divorce or she dies before she turns thirty, he gets nothing. JP also added a stipulation that as long as Samantha's boyfriend or husband is gainfully employed, then her allowance will be doubled. However, if he is not employed, then her allowance stays the same."

"Can he do that? I thought Indiana was a community property state?" Harley looked as incredulous as I felt.

"Oh yes. He can. Again, because everything is in trust, it technically doesn't belong to her yet. Now, once she turns thirty, then he will be entitled to half. But, JP didn't believe he'd stick around that long once he knew he wasn't going to have access to the money. He thought Samantha would get tired of him and it would end long before her thirtieth birthday."

A huge smile crossed Harley's face before he asked, "When do they find out?"

Not even Richard Stout could avoid laughing and I didn't try.

"I will, of course, read the will as soon as Samantha returns from her honeymoon. I think it will be a big surprise to both of them."

We left Stout's office around noon. I let Harley take my car back to the office and I walked across the street to see if Paris was free for lunch.

Most beauty salons are closed on Mondays, but Sunday is the only day Paris doesn't work. Well, at least she doesn't work at the shop. Sunday nights she caught up on her book work. She worked hard and needed to hire an accountant to help with some of the accounting and tax work. But, her last accountant was the church's minister of music who was found to be laundering money from the mob and had absconded with close to twenty thousand of her hard-earned dollars. That made her a bit reluctant to get another accountant and so she had taken back the reins of control; which meant more work and longer hours.

Un Jour a Paris' or A Day in Paris is the name of one of Paris' Salons. As the name implied, A Day in Paris was an upscale salon which offered massages, body wraps, and a host of other services I had no idea about. *Hair 2 Dye 4* was Paris' other salon. That one resembled more traditional black hair salons. Braids, perms, and sew-ins were the offerings of the day. Despite the ritzy location and upscale clientele of Un Jour a Paris, Hair 2 Dye 4 was still making more money. Apparently black women paid a lot more for their hair and were often regular clients with standing appointments from one week to the next. But, all in all, I think Paris preferred the upscale look and feel of Un Jour.

Amy, Paris' receptionist greeted me with a huge smile and a knowing wink. Her eagerness and enthusiasm were infectious. Amy was seventy-five years old and loved Paris and working for her more than just about anything else in the world, except maybe candy.

"RJ. It's so good to see you. Have a seat and I'll let Paris know you're here." Amy seemed to like me too which was another point in her favor.

She picked up the phone and told Paris I was here while simultaneously holding up a bowl of candy.

I shook my head to decline the candy and took a seat to wait. I didn't have long to wait. Paris came to the edge of the desk and motioned for me to follow her back.

Amy winked as I passed.

Un Jour a Paris was a converted warehouse with an industrial feel. Paris' office was in the back. I followed her into her office where she turned and gave me a kiss.

After a moment, she pushed away and added, "What a pleasant surprise. What brings you here?"

I noticed the half-eaten salad on her desk and added, "I came to invite you to lunch, but I see I'm too late."

"Sorry. I have an appointment in twenty minutes. Besides, aren't you supposed to be preparing for your class?"

The class Paris was referring to was the "Police, Law and Society" Class I was corralled into teaching at the local law school. I am not a professor and have never taught a class in my life. In fact, the very idea of standing in front of a classroom full of people and talking about anything was just about enough to make me want to puke. However, when Judge E.L. Browning retired from the bench to take over as Dean of the Law School, he convinced me to give it a try. Why he believed I could do this, I don't know. My first class was scheduled for this evening from six until nine. In fact, every Monday and Wednesday for the next three months, I was slated to make a fool of myself publicly. Frankly, I expected Chief Mike would say no. We were always understaffed and overworked. Initially, the class was to start at two in the afternoon. But, Chief Mike, or most likely, Mayor Longbow, thought it would be good for public relations or something. His only request was to move the time of the class back a bit and the university complied. Knowing Chief Mike as I do, he probably was afraid if I didn't teach the class, he'd be next on the judge's hit list.

"I've prepared about as much as I can." I groaned, and I had. I reviewed the lesson plan, read the books that were used last semester. I met with Judge Browning a couple of times for some last-minute pointers and even sat in on his last lecture to get some inspiration. The only thing I had achieved in all that preparing was to make myself more nervous. "I'm trying not to think about it."

Paris laughed. She had a great laugh. I found myself smiling as I looked at her. The interesting thing about dating a hair stylist, her preferred title, was that her look could change dramatically from one week to the next. In fact her hair today was different than it was yesterday. Yesterday her hair was straight and smooth. Today she was wearing it in tight spiral curls and appeared to have some Carmel highlights. Whichever way she wore her hair, it suited her and she looked good. Of course, I might be slightly biased.

"I like your hair. When did you change it?"

"This morning - I got bored."

Paris' phone rang and I knew it was Amy reporting her next appointment was here.

"I'm sorry. You didn't even get a chance to finish your lunch."

Smiling, Paris reached up and kissed me. "I'm not. If you hadn't come, I wouldn't have gotten a chance to see you before your class tonight and I wanted to wish you luck." Another kiss before she led me to the reception area. She stood smiling and waved goodbye as I left. "Call me when your class is over, professor." She smiled and greeted a young woman with dark hair that was short in the front, but had a long pink pony tail down her back.

Paris' Salon was in the basement of a building that had been converted to retail space. There was a very good restaurant upstairs that had just moved in a few weeks ago. Paris and I had eaten there many times. It had a pub atmosphere inside, but outside there were quite a few bistro tables set up. In the short period of time the *Brass Rail* had been open, it had received quite a few good reviews in the local papers and was doing well if the crowds inside were any indication. I decided to go to the bar and grab a sandwich before heading back to the station.

Harley had taken the car back to the station earlier, so I was going to get a chance to walk off the burger and fries I'd just eaten by the time I made the fifteen minute trek back to the station.

The rest of the afternoon went by much too quickly as Harley and I finished up paperwork around the murder of JP Rollins. We compared statements and made a timeline. A lot of routine paperwork and telephone calls to verify information and we weren't a great deal closer to a solution than we were forty-eight hours ago. I'd managed to talk to the police in Orlando who were keeping an eye on our newlyweds and was ensured they hadn't tried to go anywhere not on their itinerary. But all too soon, it was after five and time for me to head to the campus.

"Are you sure you don't want to come?" I had been trying to convince Harley it would be a lot of fun if we taught the class together as a team. But, he wasn't buying it.

"Ah…thanks but NO. You're on your own. Don't worry. You'll be fine." He laughed.

Mary and Joseph Catholic University (MAC-U) is a private university that was established in St. Joseph over one hundred and fifty years ago. It used to be an all male university but in the 1970's the revolution of the sexes hit and the college opened its doors to women. MAC-U was a Catholic University with a long and distinguished reputation. I can only imagine how these wealthy, pampered law students would react when they discovered their professor was just a lowly homicide cop.

MAC-U had a beautiful campus with lots of trees, old stone buildings covered with ivy and two small lakes. My class room was located in one of the newly constructed law school buildings that had just been finished about a year ago. The building was stone like the others but lacked the character of the older buildings. However, I had to admit on days like today where the temperature had gotten into the lower nineties I was extremely thankful for the modern conveniences in this new building, like elevators and air conditioning.

I hadn't even applied to MAC-U when I graduated from high school. I was a good student, but my grades certainly wouldn't have gotten me accepted. I chose instead to get away from home and go to school in the southern part of the state. Ironic that I now found myself teaching at a university I probably wouldn't have been admitted to just about a decade ago; heck, race relations being what they were, I wouldn't even have been allowed in the classroom unless I was cleaning it forty years ago. A lot can happen in a relatively short period of time.

There were forty young people of varying races and ages in my class. I started out with the administrative tasks of taking roll, going through the syllabus, books required for the course, and the grading requirements. That took thirty minutes. I answered some mundane questions about office hours and such. Then we started. I will admit I was extremely nervous. Several times, I thought there was no way I could get through this. But, by about half-way through the night, we got involved in a discussion about evidence and police procedures and that's when I really got into it. Before I knew it, there was only 1 hour left and I hadn't even given them a break. When one timid student, raised a hand and asked if we would be taking a break soon, I realized just how late it was. I expected them all to run out at break, glad to be free. But, I was surprised several of them didn't go but came down to the front of the room to continue the discussion. I looked up and noticed Judge Browning sitting in the back of the room. How long he'd been there, I don't know. He merely smiled, gave me a thumbs up and left without saying a word. The rest of the night went by quickly. After class, I had about five students who stayed to talk while I packed up and walked out to the parking lot with me. I was amazed how well things went and how comfortable I was once I got started. As I drove home at half past nine, I smiled. Perhaps this wouldn't be such a bad gig after all. I'm not sure when the thought took hold, but here were future lawyers and judges and I had a unique opportunity to shape their minds. Cops and lawyers always had a certain amount of conflict although we were all on the same side, the side of justice. But hopefully, after this class there would be forty people entering our justice system with a better understanding, and hopefully appreciation, for the role the police played in the criminal justice system. Most surprising to me was the admiration and excitement when they realized I was an actual working police officer, and not an academic. There were a lot of questions about how things are done in the '*real world*' and I was able to share examples from real cases which amazed and held their attention. But, I wasn't about to get too excited yet.

I called Paris when I got home and spent the next hour reliving the thrill. She was a great listener and extremely supportive. She even gave me some ideas for things we might do on Wednesday night. I found myself looking forward to the next class rather than dreading it. At midnight I was still too pumped up to sleep, so I decided to read ahead in my text book. That did the trick and I was asleep before I knew it.

CHAPTER 8

Exhaustion provided a few hours of sleep before the nightmares came. Thankfully, they didn't last long and I managed to get a couple more hours sleep which I considered a win over where I was a few months ago. Tuesday morning I was up bright and early and was in such a good mood I had not only made coffee by the time Harley got into the office, but had also brought two dozen donuts.

"Wow! Coffee and donuts. You are in a good mood. Class must have gone well."

I swallowed a smile. "It went okay."

"Okay? Just Okay?" He bit into a powdery donut I bought because I knew he liked them. His mouth was coated with powdered sugar and a gooey, lemon filling oozed out of the side of his mouth. His eyes rolled back into his head and he sighed.

I laughed. "Do you need a moment alone?"

He merely nodded and looked in the box to see how many more of the lemon filled donuts were left. He finished off two before he sat down to work.

Class had gone well and I was still excited. I filled him in on the details I came up with in the shower this morning. I had several ideas to make the class even more exciting, including perhaps a field trip to the station and the morgue. I bypassed the idea about getting Harley and Chief Mike to come in and answer some questions. I'd need to wait for the right time to share that one.

We went back to work. We still had a lot of work to do to nail down the timeline for the murder and also to check and cross check who was where when. It would be a lot easier if everyone told the truth but then one of the people was a murderer and since they hadn't come forward and confessed yet, they weren't likely to do so now. By general consent, we agreed to tackle the best man and two groomsmen first.

Martin Lee was the best man and according to his statement he was currently unemployed, so we went to his apartment. Fortunately for us, his roommate, Ryan Harris was also one of the groomsmen, so we could save time and interview together.

Martin Lee and Ryan Harris were in their early twenties and looked, dressed, and acted like frat boys. They lived in a two bedroom apartment that looked and smelled like it hadn't been cleaned in months. The walls were probably white at one time or another but with all of the scuff marks it was hard to tell. There were about two weeks worth of dirty clothes strewn across every piece of furniture amongst empty beer cans, pizza boxes and bags from fast food restaurants. Ryan answered the door in flip flops wearing a pair of shorts with a beer in hand. Martin was sitting on a pile of clothes that must have been covering a sofa and playing a video game.

"We'd like to talk to you?" I flashed my shield.

Ryan tried his best to hide the label of the beer can with his hand. "Sure. Come on in. You're the cops...ah...I mean you're the police we talked to on Saturday." Ryan stepped aside and kicked a few items out of the way, so we could enter the room.

Martin looked up briefly from his game, nodded and kept playing.

Harley stepped in front of the set until Martin looked up. "Perhaps you wouldn't mind pausing your game and answering a few questions for us."

"Sure. Yeah." Martin groaned as his player was killed.

Based on the empty glazed look in his eyes, he didn't appear to be the brightest bulb in the pack. However, he put the game control down.

"We would like to hear what happened at the wedding and reception from both of you." I looked from one to the other and waited.

Harley looked around for a place to sit, but decided instead to stand as he took his notepad out and began taking notes.

Ryan and Martin exchanged looks, but then shrugged and scowled as if the events of a marriage and murder just three days ago were so common place it would take great effort and emotion to summon up the images.

Ryan was probably the brighter of the two. He shrugged. "Well, we had a late night the Friday night before." Here a smile of remembrance brightened his expression for a second. He glanced at Harley and me; our stone-faced glares sobered him up to the seriousness of the situation and he continued. "We had a bachelor's party for Todd and were out really late. I don't think we got back until maybe three. Then we crashed."

"Where was that?" Harley asked.

"Here." Martin added as if it should have been obvious. Who wouldn't want to stay in this filthy hole in the wall?

I nodded for him to continue.

Ryan rubbed the back of his neck and thought for a moment before continuing. "We didn't get much sleep because Sam wanted us at the church by eight. She called every ten minutes from like six-thirty until eight-fifteen to make sure we were up and getting Todd dressed.

Martin looked his annoyance, *like how dare she expect the groom to arrive on time at the church.* "So we got up and threw some clothes on and got to the church about nine or so. And, then we got dressed for the wedding."

"What time did the wedding start?" I asked even though I already knew the answer.

"Ten-thirty" was Martin's contribution.

Ryan must have either forgotten we were there or forgot he was too young to legally drink alcohol and took a sip of his beer before continuing. "Then the wedding started. It was all over by eleven-fifteen. We had to take a boat load of pictures."

"Was this at the church?" I asked.

"Yeah - most of them were at the church, and then we went to the American Legion and took some there. Although, we got thirsty by then and it was sort of hard to get everyone at the same place for the pictures." Ryan and Martin looked at each other and laughed.

Harley stared. "So, the drinking started up again pretty early?"

"Yeah, open bar, man it was great. Todd said he wanted to drink the old buzzard dry and we were welcome to help." Martin and Ryan laughed although Ryan caught on a bit quicker that perhaps they weren't portraying their friend in the best light and added, "yeah, but you know Todd didn't mean any harm in it. It was just fun...you know?"

Actually, I didn't know, and didn't look as if I did.

Ryan sighed. "So, then we were all drinking and dancing and doing shots. Some people ate. The photographer kept trying to get us to take pictures. I think he got some but once the drinking started...it was a bit crazy."

"Where did you do all of this drinking?" I asked trying not to sound as disgusted as I felt.

"All over. I think we started out in the main room, but we had to keep moving to get away from the photographer. We got a bottle of Jack Daniels and went out back."

Ryan shook his head. Perhaps even he couldn't believe how he'd behaved.

"Man that was some party. It was the best reception ever. I mean all the booze you can drink. And we can drink some booze." Ryan grinned and then let out a belch which merely caused him to smile.

Alright I was wrong, he had no clue he'd behaved badly in any way whatsoever.

"Where was Mr. Rollins when all this was happening?" Harley brought them back to the main point.

They exchanged another look and Martin added, "Man, he was right there with us. I thought the old man was some kind of crank, but there he was taking Jager bombs and doing all kinds of shots along with us. That old man could really knock it back," admiration from Martin.

"So, Mr. Rollins was right there with you the whole time?" I tried to clarify.

"Well..not the *whole* time. Like I said, if you stayed in one place too long, that photographer was all over you. But, he drank quite a bit." Martin strained to remember, but shook his head and apparently gave up trying.

Ryan continued. "The photographer wanted pictures of the bride dancing with her father or uncle or whatever he was. So, they started dancing, but they'd both had too much to drink and were slipping and sliding all over the place. It was hilarious." Ryan and Martin both laughed at the recollection. Then, Ryan pulled himself together enough to add, "That's when the old guy fell."

"He fell? I don't remember anyone mentioning that." I looked at Harley and he confirmed by shaking his head.

"Yeah, he fell when they were dancing. Me and Tyler had to help him to the back to lie down." Ryan added.

"It's Tyler and I," I said without thinking.

His blood shot eyes looked confused. "What?"

"Never mind. So, you and Tyler helped him to the back, then what? Did anyone else go back there?" I asked

Shrugs and head shakes were all they could muster.

I must have looked incredulous because Martin added, "hey, we weren't exactly following the old man around or anything. We were enjoying the party. Who knew he'd go and get himself murdered?"

Neither guy remembered much that would be considered helpful including times when they went to or near the back room. Yes they went to the bathroom at some point, but neither one had the slightest inkling of when. Thirty minutes of questions and a lot of blank looks later, we were all frustrated. Harley and I were frustrated at their lack of understanding of the gravity of the situation or the fact they didn't seem to care that a fellow human being was dead. Martin and Ryan were frustrated with having to answer questions they thought were pointless; and probably frustrated at being kept from their video game by cops trying to solve the murder of the man who funded their last alcoholic binge.

I was tired of standing and noticed for the first time that Harley was engrossed in watching a pair of dirty boxers as they inched across the floor. That was the last straw.

"If you think of anything else, please call us." I almost handed them a business card, but realized it would just end up as one more thing lost in that sea of clutter. Harley snapped out of his trance and stepped over a few items as we left.

In the hallway, "RJ, did you see that? Those shorts started moving across the floor. I kept trying to see what was under there, but I couldn't. You think it was a rat?"

"Wouldn't surprise me."

"Geez, I thought I was going to have to get my gun and shoot it." Harley kept looking back at the apartment as we headed out as if he expected the boxers to follow us.

"I don't know how anyone can live in that filth."

"That place is creepy." Harley shuddered. "I feel like I need a bath." He shook himself like a wet dog.

We resisted the urge to go home and bathe; and decided instead to go and talk to the last groomsman and the maid of honor.

Kelly and Tyler Lyston, in addition to having the honor of holding prominent positions in the wedding as maid of honor and groomsman, were also the groom's cousins. They lived in a trailer on the outskirts of town.

Kelly was about twenty-one, medium height with cobalt blue hair that she wore in a buzz cut. As bizarre as it sounds, it actually looked good on her. She was tattooed and pierced in so many places I wondered if she had trouble going through metal detectors at the airport. She must have had fifteen or twenty holes in each ear, three rings were in each eyebrow, and she had a tongue bar and a naval ring was clearly visible between her hip hugging Daisy Dukes and midriff tank.

Tyler was much more sedate. He shaved his head, preferring instead to use his scalp to display his numerous tattoos. He too had a ton of body piercings. Tyler was outside working on a car that was up on cement blocks while Kelly read a magazine while she sat on a toilet under a tree in the yard. She wasn't using the facilities, but merely used the porcelain throne for additional seating.

As Harley and I approached, we automatically started taking visual note of our surroundings. Not that living in a trailer automatically meant you were not a law abiding citizen. But we'd both recognized this particular trailer park as the place that one of our fellow officers was shot to death a few months ago when coming to serve a warrant.

As we walked, Harley told me he'd been called out several times for domestic disputes. Nothing ever made it to court, but it made us both cautious.

As we approached, Tyler wiped grease from his hands and stared.

I decided to try to make sure this encounter stayed friendly. "Nice car. That's a 1963 Ford Falcon convertible isn't it?"

Tyler looked impressed as he nodded. "You want to buy it?"

"Is it for sale?" I didn't even try to hide the excitement in my voice nor the admiration in my face. I love cars and classic cars are a thing of beauty, working or not. I drive a Toyota Camry. But, my 1959 Eldorado was my baby.

"It might be for the right price." Tyler's shoulders relaxed as he watched me admiring the car.

"How long you been working on her?"

"Two years too long." Kelly added, not bothering to rise from her seat. "But you didn't come way out here to admire a piece of crap that don't work and probably never will. You're those cops from the wedding ain't you?"

"Yes. We need to ask a few more questions." Harley smiled. "Where're you from?" He commented on Kelly's southern accent.

"Mississippi. Where you from? You ain't from around these parts with that accent."

"Tennessee." Harley smiled.

They nodded, each acknowledging their common confederate bond.

Thinking back, I remembered Harley had been interviewing the kitchen staff while I interviewed the wedding party. So, he hadn't been involved in the initial interview with Mrs. Lyston. This was the first time he'd had an opportunity to talk to his fellow southerner.

"Yeah. I remember you guys." Tyler looked jittery. "What kind of questions?" Tyler seemed more reluctant than his wife to talk. However, he knew my admiration of his car wasn't feigned and that gave us a bond, however slight. I truly do love cars and the Ford Falcon is an amazing piece of machinery.

"You must know Todd and Samantha pretty well." I said.

"Known Todd my whole life. He's my cousin," Tyler added as he went back to tinkering under the hood.

"How about Samantha?" Harley looked at Kelly. "I mean she picked you as Maid of Honor."

Without words being spoken, Harley and I had silently decided to work each one separately. He would talk to Kelly and I would talk to Tyler. Perhaps if they weren't paying attention to each other's conversations and were instead, focusing on their own answers, they might give us some information we wouldn't get otherwise.

"I introduced them. Me and Tyler been married about three years. I knew Todd from family gatherings. I met Samantha when we were taking a class at the community college. We hit it off right away and I didn't even know her old man was rich." She added with pride.

"How long ago was that?" Harley took out his notepad and started taking notes.

"About six months ago."

Harley dropped his pen, but recovered well as he stood up again he was able to ask calmly, "Samantha and Todd have only known each other for six months?"

Fortunately, Kelly didn't seem to think there was anything unusual in marrying someone you'd only known for six months because she added, "Yup. Isn't that romantic? It was like love at first sight just like on television."

"Yeah, it certainly is…" Harley wrote. "Did you notice anything unusual at the reception?"

Tyler and I talked about the car and he had loosened up a bit. So, I asked in a casual tone, "What did you think about Todd marrying into all that money?"

Tyler kept tinkering, but then he mumbled, "Thought he was making a fool of himself. He thought he was going to be rich. But, rich folks like that make sure poor folks like us don't get any of their money. I told him so."

"How was Todd thinking he'd get the money?" I asked as casually as you can while hanging over an engine.

Tyler tinkered with the engine a few seconds and then stood up and wiped his hands. Looking at me, he added "Look, if you want me to say Todd killed that old man, you're wasting your time. He may not be the smartest dog in the pack, but he ain't THAT stupid. He didn't kill nobody."

"I'm not accusing him of anything. I'm just trying to understand what happened. It helps us if we can get a feel for who the people are. We don't know Todd and Samantha. I'm sure they're fine people. But, someone killed JP Rollins in the middle of his daughter's wedding reception. We're just trying to find out what you might have seen or heard that might help us figure this thing out."

Tyler Lyston looked at me for a few seconds then shrugged his shoulders and bent back over and continued tinkering with the engine. He mumbled and I bent down to hear.

"I don't know nothin."

I overheard Kelly talking to Harley about the beautiful white dress she got to wear. "I thought it was a bit strange. You know, the bride is the one who wears the white dress. So, if she wore white and then wanted us all to wear white too…well, that's just a lot of white, you know. But, then she must have known all along she was going to wear red. It was AWESOME. Just like a freakin' fairy tale. It was like Cinderella or something. Here was Todd, so poor he didn't even have a pot to pee in." Perhaps the irony of the situation hit her as she realized here she was sitting on a toilet as she made that comment, because she suddenly started laughing.

"A pot to pee in…get it?" She laughed, pointing to her toilet.

Harley nodded, "Yes, I get it."

Tyler stood up suddenly and yelled, "shut up! You don't know what you're talkin' 'bout half the time no way. Always got your nose in some stupid magazine."

This was obviously an old argument because Kelly merely sniffed, rolled her eyes and turned her head.

Tyler leaned back down and continued his tinkering. I wasn't going to get anything more out of him. He'd shut down. Harley and I exchanged looks and a slight nod so subtle I doubt if anyone noticed.

"Well, if you think of anything else that might help, please call us." I heard Harley saying as he handed Kelly a business card. She held on to it as if he'd given her a hundred-dollar bill.

"Wow. These are cool. I always wanted to work at a job where we got business cards." Looking defiantly over at her husband, she stuck out her chin. "And, someday I will, even if I have to join the police force to do it." However, the dramatics were lost on Tyler who grunted and continued tinkering.

Kelly whispered in a voice you'd have to be deaf not to hear, "Some people don't want anything more than what they got, which ain't jack and they'll never amount to nothin.'"

Another grunt from under the hood was the only response she got.

She reached down the front of her shirt and tucked the card in her bra and then continued reading her magazine.

Harley and I headed back to the car and left.

We decided to grab a bite to eat at The Ice Box. The Ice Box is a small hamburger joint located near campus. The décor consisted mostly of MAC-U Hockey memorabilia. The University had a decent hockey team, although I'm not into hockey, I knew they'd won a conference title last year and were hoping to make it a national title this year.

As Harley bit into his burger he asked, "So what did you think? Sounds like Todd was planning on coming into some money."

"It's something, but I'm thinking maybe he wasn't the only one who was expecting to come into some money."

Between chews, "What do you mean?"

"What about the girl...Kelly? She seemed a bit of a social climber. Maybe she thought if Todd came into money, he'd share the wealth with his cousin and, by default, her. Or maybe there was something going on between her and Todd."

"Maybe Samantha did it along with the husband. She certainly didn't seem to have any love for her old man."

"Lots of maybes are about all we've got at the moment. But, it's possible. I suppose anyone of them could have done it. It might be something totally unrelated too."

Harley stopped the burger midway to his mouth. "What do you mean?"

"I think we need to look further into his business dealings. Anyone with that much money and his reputation for wanting to have everything his own way is bound to have made enemies along the way."

The Ice Box burgers were large and juicy, but my favorite item on the menu was the fries. They were seasoned fries and nice and salty, just the way I liked them.

Harley took another bite of his burger. "Still a lot of maybes."

"We need to find someone who knows all of the people involved and can give us some answers about them."

"What about Paris?"

"She was just working. She didn't really *KNOW* them, but I'll ask her tonight. Maybe she heard something that might help."

"What about the lawyer?"

"He's worth a try. Maybe he can give us a name. We should start with him."

We finished eating our lunch and headed back to the Old Waterman Building in the hopes that Richard Stout would be able to see us.

We caught a break and he was not only in the office, but he had fifteen minutes and was willing to spend them with us.

"What can I do for you gentlemen today?"

I sat down in the chair he offered. "We have a few more questions we'd like to ask if you don't mind.

Harley sat and pulled out his notepad.

"Not at all. Anything I can do to help."

I started with an easy question. "Did JP Rollins have any enemies?"

I wasn't expecting the laughter and it took me by surprise. Harley and I exchanged glances.

Stout worked to regain his composure. "I'm sorry gentlemen. I don't know why that struck me as funny. I realize this is a serious matter. But, JP Rollins made enemies everywhere he went, everyday of the week."

"Explain." I said.

"Well, JP was very abrasive and controlling. Anyone who stood in his way either had to move or get stepped on. Once, there was a piece of land he wanted to buy. There was a little old lady who owned a house smack dab in the middle of the plot he wanted. And she refused to sell. You'd think he would have given up. There's tons of land all over he could have bought. But, it just made JP mad."

"What did he do about it?" Harley asked.

"He bought all the property around her and built the ugliest structure money could buy up to the very edge of her property line. He built so high it blocked out the sun and left her with virtually no light. It was noisy and smelly and there were trucks coming and going at all times of the day and night. Those trucks shook her house every time they passed by." He shook his head in recollection. "When she couldn't take it anymore and agreed to sell, he refused to buy it. Told her he didn't need her house anymore. Poor old woman had to move into a nursing home, her nerves were so bad. The house went into foreclosure and that's when he bought it for less than half what it was worth."

Harley realized his mouth was hanging open and closed it before adding, "Didn't anyone try to stop him?"

"People tried. Her kids tried taking him to court, but he had more money and more time. All he had to do was keep delaying and delaying until she either died or gave up."

I didn't like JP Rollins from the moment I heard he made a pass at Paris. Now, I really didn't like him. Fortunately, or unfortunately, it doesn't matter whether we liked someone or not. Our job was to solve the murder. But I couldn't help wondering if perhaps someone had done the world a service when they ended JP Rollins' life.

Stout continued, "JP Rollins was a force to be reckoned with."

I looked a little more carefully at Richard Stout, attorney for JP Rollins. He worked for a man he clearly disliked. "Yet you worked for him."

Stout swiveled around in his chair and looked out the window for about 30 seconds before adding. "Yes. I worked for him" was all he said.

"Did JP Rollins make the kind of enemies that would want to stick a knife in his chest?" I asked although I already guessed the answer.

"Most of his enemies, business associates, family and some of his friends would have gladly plunged that knife into his chest. JP was the kind of man you either hated or truly despised. I can think of ten or fifteen people that will come to the funeral just to spit on his grave.

I took a second to think before asking, "What about you?"

Richard Stout didn't immediately answer. I almost repeated the question but decided to wait him out. Maybe a minute passed before stout added, "I suppose you can add me to that list. JP was an excellent businessman but he had a cruel streak."

Harley asked as if merely wondering out loud, "So why did you continue working for him?"

Stout got up and paced around the office. He paused and then put on a half-smile before adding as if in a daze, "When you sell your soul to the devil, you have to pay the price. There's no walking away no matter how much I..." Stout stopped here and shook himself as if to shake off the regretful mood he'd allowed to show. Once again in control of his thoughts and actions, Stout added in a brighter tone, "I'm sorry gentlemen but I do have a client coming shortly."

"Maybe you could give us a list of the top five or ten individuals who not only hated JP Rollins but would have wanted him dead; if any of them were at the wedding that would be better." I added as Harley and I rose to leave.

Stout agreed to work on it and we made our departure.

"Geez! Can you believe that?" Harley added as we got into the car and headed back to the station.

"Doesn't look like JP Rollins will be missed very much if his lawyer is telling the truth."

"You don't believe him?"

"It's not that I don't believe him. I just want to know if maybe he's trying to steer us away from himself. Too many suspects are just as bad as too few."

"For someone as well known as JP Rollins, it shouldn't be too difficult to get information on him." I looked at Harley. "You hit the files when we get back to the station and see what you can find out."

He nodded. "What are you going to do?"

"I think I know someone who might be able to give us a little more on JP Rollins and his business dealings."

Judge E.L. Browning retired from the bench just a few months ago. But he wasn't ready for a rocking chair yet. Instead, he had taken over as dean of MAC-U's Law School. As one of the prominent figures in St. Joe, he was also still very active on the boards of several businesses. If anyone knew about JP Rollins' business dealings, it was Judge Browning.

E.L.'s home was something of a surprise to me the first time I visited. I expected a prominent member of the political, legal and business community to live in one of the big mansions that lined George Washington Avenue. GW Avenue was a wide tree lined street with massive brick and stone homes set back from the street with huge lawns. Instead, E.L. lived in an area of town local folk called *Pill Hill*. Pill Hill was once the place to be for successful African-Americans in St. Joseph. In fact the nickname was coined because of the number of doctors who lived in the area. Pill Hill was a winding area of medium sized homes built in the 1940's and 1950's. Judge Browning lived in a mid-century modern home built around 1955's. The one-story ranch was what I would call a rambler. It had a couple of additions that made it larger than it appeared from the street. However, the truly remarkable thing about E.L. Browning's home was not the home itself, but the grounds. While Pill Hill didn't have the massive lawns of GW Avenue, a few of the homes were built on oversized or double lots. Judge Brwoning's home was one of them. The yard was landscaped in a Japanese style that had won many awards over the years and was one of the last stops on the

St. Joseph Garden Walk each year. The gardens were not due to the judge's green thumb, but were the result of his housekeeper, gardener, cook, former nurse, and I suspected his girlfriend. When E.L.'s wife Carol was diagnosed with cancer almost twenty years ago, He hired a young Japanese woman named Hiroko to help care for her. Hiroko nursed and cared for Carol for five long years. After Carol's death, Hiroko stayed on. I wondered if there was more to the relationship between Hiroko and E.L., but hadn't been bold enough to ask. Hiroko's influence was seen in the Japanese gardens, the interior décor and also in the low furnishings that adorned the house. However, there were never any demonstrations of affection to confirm my suspicions and it was none of my business.

I rang the door bell and it was Hiroko who answered.

She smiled and bowed as she recognized me and then in her broken English, "He in study. You go."

I stepped inside and removed my shoes, which made Hiroko smile. I bowed and thanked her and walked back to the room that E.L. set aside for his study.

While minimalist Asian design reigned in the Browning home, E.L.'s office was apparently exempt from the influence. Here, he had a comfortable male retreat. Dark wood, leather and books dominated the space. The rest of the house was Asian inspired, but this was an English gentleman's country library. The large room had floor to ceiling book shelves on three of the four walls that were crammed full of books. A massive mahogany desk sat in the middle of the floor and that's where I found E.L.

"RJ what a pleasant surprise. To what do I owe this pleasure? You come to sign up to teach a couple more classes for next semester?" He invited me to sit as he leaned back in his chair.

I smiled. "I just want to get through this one."

"Oh come now. I stuck my head in and saw how well you were doing. I knew you'd be an awesome teacher."

I could hear the pride as he spoke and it shone clear in his eyes. I was honored to see how much he thought of me. "It went better than I expected, but that was only the first night. I've got a lot more nights to go. I wouldn't get too excited yet."

"I'm not worried in the least. I believe in you. You just needed to believe in yourself. That's all."

"Thanks." I shook my head. "It wasn't the horrible nightmare I thought it would be but I'm not planning to quit my day job... well, not for teaching anyway."

He gave me a puzzled stare, but when I didn't elaborate, he let it go. So far only a handful of people knew I was thinking about retiring from the police. The nightmares weren't as bad as they were right after the accident, but they were still there. I'd considered quitting the force, but had grown accustomed to eating. When Chief Mike gave me the option of becoming a consultant, I started to think of life beyond the police force. If I were a consultant and a part time teacher, I could definitely support myself, but I needed to mull it over a little more, but now wasn't the time. "I actually came to pick your brain about something,"

E.L. looked intrigued and then extended his arm as if to say, *go ahead*.

Before I could continue, there was a brief knock on the door and Hiroko entered with a Tea Tray. She placed the tea on the edge of the desk, bowed and then left the room, closing the door after herself.

E.L. came around to the front of the desk and poured both of us a cup of tea and then took the seat next to me and waited.

"I know you sit on the boards of several companies and are familiar with a number of important people. I was wondering what you can tell me about JP Rollins." I sipped my tea and watched his face.

"I heard about his death. I'll admit I didn't like the man, but I wouldn't wish that fate on anyone."

"From what I hear, you may be one of the only people in town who wouldn't."

"He didn't have a lot of friends. JP Rollins was one of those men who scratched and clawed his way to the top. And, heaven help you if you got in his way."

"Anyone in particular get in his way?"

He took a moment to think while he drank his tea. "You mean business associates?"

"I mean anyone who hated him enough to kill him."

"Well, there were two people who come immediately to mind."

I waited expectantly but was still surprised by what came next.

"His partner and his wife."

I had just taken a drink of tea and almost spit it out. "Wife? JP Rollins was married?" I couldn't even pretend to hide my amazement.

"Oh yeah. He was married."

"We didn't find anything about a wife. Why didn't anyone tell us? His lawyer said he didn't have any other family besides the niece."

"JP Rollins was married about twenty-some odd years ago. But his wife had an affair with his business partner. JP found out about it and boy was he furious."

"I'll bet he was. From what I've heard about him, I can't believe he didn't try and kill them."

E.L. chuckled before adding, "He did." He paused long enough for the shock to resonate in my brain before continuing. "He shot the partner, but only managed to wing him before he high tailed it out the nearest window. Tossed the wife out of the house with nothing but the clothes on her back."

I realized then that my mouth was hanging open and closed it, but after a few seconds I opened it again to ask, "What happened to them?"

E.L. took a sip of tea. "He destroyed the business partner. JP Rollins literally black-balled him. He was a very successful and influential man. He pulled his business and money away from anyone who continued to do business with the partner." E.L. shook his head. "Poor guy couldn't get any contracts, no loans, nothing. He ended up filing for bankruptcy. No one was willing to risk the wrath of JP Rollins. Eventually, he just sort of shriveled up and shrank away. Died later in a car accident."

"But how is this possible? Why didn't someone mention this before now?"

Leaning back in his chair, E.L. sipped his tea and said, "Well there may not be a lot of people who remember. It was a long time ago. But anyone who brought up the subject suddenly found themselves on the wrong side of JP Rollins and that was a very dangerous place to be."

"What about the wife? What happened to her?"

"Dead. She died in the same car accident that killed the partner."

Something in E.L.'s voice alerted me there was something more. Pondering his words I realized that having two tragic car accidents was a bit of a coincidence.

"Wait. Wait. Didn't his brother die in a car accident too?"

E.L. nodded.

"You can't be serious. His wife dies in a car accident. His business partner dies in a car accident and his brother?" It took a moment, but then the light bulb came on. "His brother WAS his business partner?"

E.L. nodded.

"But that would mean…You mean his brother and his wife?" I was incredulous and found myself pacing the office.

"The original company was called Rollins Brothers Trucking and Rollins Brothers Rentals. After the unfortunate affair, no pun intended, JP changed the name of the company and shut his brother out of everything."

"But he adopted his niece? Oh this is all twisted. So, his niece is his step daughter? He adopted her." I was shaking my head in the hopes it might clear up this mess.

"No. JP never divorced his wife."

I must have looked as stupid as I felt, because EL waited a minute and then added, "He never adopted the girl. He didn't have to. By law, the girl may not have been his biological child but she was his child in the eyes of the court. He was still married to her mother."

"Wow. So, does the daughter…ah…I mean the niece know any of this?"

E.L. shrugged and poured more tea. Holding up the pot, I shook my head declining a refill.

"I don't know who would be brave enough to tell her, but I can't imagine she's lived in this small town this long and hasn't run across some busy body who hasn't at least hinted at the truth."

"Any possibility JP was responsible for the crash?" I wondered.

"No. He had an iron tight alibi at the time and trust me, he would have been one of the first people the police would have looked at. There was never any suspicion he had anything to do with the car accident."

"But, why keep the girl? I mean if he was as evil as that, why did he take her in and raise her? Surely there was someone else who could have taken her?"

"I'm sure JP was the only person who can answer that question. It doesn't appear he was cruel to her." Pausing, E.L. waited a moment, and then shrugged before adding, "Well, he certainly wasn't any crueler to her than he was to anyone else. As to why he did it? I have no idea."

"But this is bizarre. Why wasn't any of this in the police file?"

"What crime was committed?" E.L. continued to sip his tea and added, "Apart from being cruel hearted and unforgiving? Fortunately or unfortunately, that's not a crime."

As I drove back to the station later I still had difficulty sorting through everything E.L. had told me. JP Rollins actions may not have been criminal, but they certainly provided a great motive for murder. Revenge.

Sometimes I feel like I'm almos' gone

Sometimes I feel like I'm almos' gone

Sometimes I feel like I'm almos' gone

Way up in de heab'nly land

Way up in de heab'nly land

True believer

Way up in de heab'nly land

Way up in de heab'nly land

CHAPTER 9

I filled Harley in on the information I learned from Judge Browning when I got back to the station and we got to work tracking down information on the wife, the brother and any other details we could find. A few hours later, I had to leave to pick up Mama B and Paris.

Paris and Mama B were both on the Pastor's Anniversary Committee. Rev. Hilton V. Hamilton had been the pastor of First Baptist Church for forty-five years, a huge milestone. Like many marriages, the numbers of pastors that leave their first love, the church, were increasing. As the old guard gave way to younger pastors, the average stay had diminished considerably. Whether by choice or by force, many younger pastors didn't seem to have the same stamina or fortitude to go the distance. However, we were extremely blessed to have the leadership and guidance of Rev. Hamilton and intended to show him so in a big way at the festivities.

The Pastor's Anniversary was always a big affair with a week of activities. However, this year would be bigger than ever before. Everyone was asked to contribute forty-five dollars toward the anniversary, one dollar for each year of service. And, surprisingly enough almost everyone had complied. In addition, each auxiliary, Ushers, choirs, mother's board, were all raising money to try and outdo each other in their group donations. From what I heard from Paris and Mama B, these groups were extremely competitive and some had actually been hosting concerts and events for months to raise money.

Both Paris and Mama B were on the Anniversary Committee and were meeting to arrange the program. Paris was representing the choirs, in the absence of a permanent minister of music. The anniversary was only a week away and the committee was now in a wild frenzy, ironing out last minute details. The committee was meeting tonight at the church, after which the children's choir and drill team were having a program in a last ditch effort to raise money.

The youth ministry at the church had increased substantially over the past years, somewhat due to the success of our late Choir Director. The Children's Choir and Youth Choir were popular in African American churches. The junior ushers, drill team, sign choir and praise dancers were relatively new additions. Many churches had Drill Teams which performed choreographed routines with military-like precision while reciting scriptures. There were even competitions for the drill teams. FBC's drill team placed second over the summer in a city-wide competition; and was excited about the possibility of competing at the state trials later this year.

I arrived at the church in time to see the last routine of the Drill Team as they marched, in fatigues and combat boots out of the church to a standing ovation of parents, family members, and friends. As they left, I found Mama B and slid in beside her. She was wearing a cool, lightweight suit in a soft lilac with a matching lilac beret. It was tilted rather rakishly to the side and affixed to her head with a large lilac tipped hat pin.

"You're late." She whispered.

I gave her a kiss on the cheek and whispered in her ear, "I was working."

She looked as if she didn't believe me, but handed me a peppermint anyway.

The performance lasted about two hours and was an overwhelming success. For the cost of admission, ten dollars, we received an excellent performance from the youth of the church and dinner. The dinner was largely what would be called a potluck. The youth hit up almost every woman in the church to bring in a dish. Paris made a Taco Salad that was excellent and large enough to feed an army, while Mama B brought a couple of pound cakes. I love Mama B's pound cake. She literally adds a pound of butter, sugar, flour and eggs. You can almost feel your arteries clogging with each bite, but it's a wonderful way to go. There was definitely a unique variety of salads, entrees and desserts. As a single man, women assume I can't cook and must be on the verge of starvation. So, I found myself plied with everything from spaghetti to meatballs to greens and fried chicken. It was truly an international meal and by the time I managed to get Mama B and Paris out of there, I was stuffed like a Thanksgiving Turkey. Everything I ate tasted good although not all cooks are created equal. Mama B was still my favorite but there were definitely a lot of contenders for second place.

At Mama B's, Paris and I went inside for a few moments, which turned out to be a couple of hours. Mama B loved to talk and she loved company, so if you stopped you would definitely be there at least an hour or her feelings were hurt. But, fortunately, Paris loved Mama B as much as I did. Visitors were entertained and well fed if nothing else.

Paris and I sat on the sofa closest to Mama B's favorite chair. Mama B rocked in her beat up, leather rocker. It had once been green, but now was sweat stained and patched with tape. However, Mama B loved that chair, even though it had most certainly seen better days.

Paris was still excited about the performance which was evident in her voice, "I love the sign choir and watching those babies perform."

Mama B sniffed and continued to rock.

Paris wasn't about to concede there was a human being on the planet who could resist those angelic little faces. She also knew Mama B well enough to know she was a lot of talk but was a softie deep down inside.

"Oh don't tell me you didn't love seeing them sign to '*I Want to be a Christian in my Heart*.' That was so precious." Paris challenged.

Reluctantly Mama B chuckled. "I didn't say they weren't cute." She rocked. "But, the idea of a sign choir is ridiculous. Who ever heard of such nonsense? If someone was deaf, why do they need a sign choir?"

I decided to stay out of this argument due in part to the fact I agreed with Mama B. When Minister Warrendale, our former

Choir Director and Minister of Music, first suggested a Sign Choir, I thought it was crazy.

"Well, I won't say I didn't think it was a bit silly myself, at first" Paris reluctantly admitted, but quickly added "however, I can see the benefit now. Just because someone is deaf, doesn't mean they can't enjoy the beat or the lyrical beauty of the performance. They're going to want to know what the choir is singing about, even if they can't hear the words."

Mama B sniffed and continued to rock.

Paris turned to me for support. "Don't you agree RJ?"

I tried to turn away, but she made a point to look me in the eyes before adding, "You can't mean you don't like the Sign Choir?" She sounded so disappointed, I actually felt guilty.

"I didn't say I don't like the choir. I do. I think they're cute. But..."

"But what?"

Reluctantly, "It's just there aren't any deaf people who attend service? If someone was deaf and attended FBC it might make more sense to me to have a sign choir."

Paris looked me in the eyes for a full minute before busting out laughing. "Ok. I guess you're right about that. But I just think those little kids are so cute and they worked so hard to learn to sign. Plus, it's a skill they can always use."

Mama B looked at us as we sparred back and forth with a tenderness that made me a little embarrassed. Paris and I had only been dating for a few months and the relationship was pretty new. We were still feeling each other out, dancing around like two boxers at the start of a fight; we were figuring out each other's weaknesses and strengths. Obviously, Mama B had already decided we were destined to spend the rest of our lives together. And, I can't say the idea hadn't crossed my mind a time or two. But, who knew what might happen by the later rounds.

"What kind of skill are you talking about?" I joked.

"Well, if they ever meet a deaf person, they'll be able to communicate with them." Paris added smugly.

"Yeah, they can sign, *I Want to Be a Christian in My Heart*." Mama B added, flailing her arms around as she rocked.

We laughed. Mama B had a way of making people laugh. She never cared for our flamboyant former choir director who introduced the sign choir, but she loved the kids and always supported them.

Paris gave up. "Well, I like the sign choir and if we ever do have deaf people join the church, I'm sure they will feel comforted to see the choir."

Mama B sniffed at that, but didn't argue.

We stayed a bit longer and talked and laughed and then Paris said she had to get home. She had an appointment early tomorrow morning and needed to get some rest.

Mama B had apparently made each of us a small loaf of pound cake to take home. So, with our pound cakes in tow, we made our exit.

Paris had gotten a ride to the church with one of the stylists at her salon, *Hair 2 Dye 4*, knowing I would bring her home.

Paris and I actually lived within walking distance of each other. But our neighborhoods were separated by the St. Joseph River. My townhouse was on one side of the river while her one hundred-year-old Georgian home was on the other. Pulling up to the front, I helped her out of the car and walked her to the front door, holding her pound cake while she opened the door.

"Do you want to come in and have some tea and pound cake?" She asked.

My response was physical rather than verbal, and when she came up for air, we went inside.

Paris' was renovating an old home with high ceilings, fantastic woodwork, about eight fireplaces and a great view of the St. Joseph River from the back of the house. Her kitchen was one of the few rooms she had actually completed and was one of my favorite places.

I turned on some jazz while she prepared the tea. She had a large island in the middle of her kitchen where I loved to sit and watch her cook.

"I want to ask you something about JP Rollins murder."

She looked around and scanned my face before shrugging, "Sure. Ask away."

"Did you see or hear anything suspicious?" I was deliberately vague, not wanting to lead her in any direction, but preferred to have her volunteer information.

She looked puzzled as she continued getting cups and plates and placing them on the island. Finally, she stood still and thought. "It would be easier if I knew what you were wanting."

"I don't want to influence you. I'm just wondering if anyone said or did anything that was unusual or strange."

"Like sticking a knife in someone's chest?"

"I mean anything. Did anything that happened Saturday strike you as odd?"

She shrugged. "Almost everything about that wedding struck me as odd—from the dress to the makeup. It was all strange."

The kettle whistled and she went to turn it off. She filled our cups, and then sat down and thought. After a few moments she said, "Most women have planned their wedding day since they were little girls. It's the one time when you're the center of attention and can truly look and act like a princess." She sipped her tea. "So I thought it was strange JP Rollins was so involved in the details. Most men just aren't that into the details." She thought a few more moments. "It was obvious she didn't really like him a lot. That seemed strange to me. I mean, whether he was her father or her uncle, he was still family. He was the family that was paying for the whole thing."

"Did they argue?"

"Not really." She tilted her head and thought. "I think she did things she knew would irritate him on purpose, like showing up late. He ranted and complained but she just went on about her way as if to say, 'you can't control me.'"

"Anything else?"

She hesitated. "I don't know if it's really important or not…"

"Anything you saw or heard—it doesn't matter how insignificant."

She sighed. "I got the impression the groom was…cheating."

"Already?"

"I don't have any proof, but when Samantha wasn't looking

or when he *thought* she wasn't looking, I noticed some glances between the groom and one of the bridesmaids."

"Which one?"

"I don't know her name, but she had blond hair with copper highlights."

"Natalie? Are you sure?"

"No. I'm not sure. I told you it was more of an impression... nothing concrete. I didn't see them doing anything."

"No. I mean, are you sure it was the blond and not the one with the blue buzz cut and all the piercings and tattoos?"

Paris looked puzzled, but shook her head. "I don't think so. Why? Was he sleeping with her too?"

"No. I mean I don't know. There just seems to be something a little off with that one. I can't put my finger on it. But, that doesn't matter. So, you're saying you got the impression there was something between the groom and the bridesmaid?"

"I think so, but it might not mean anything. I mean maybe if Samantha was the one that got killed it might matter, but how can it matter to JP Rollins' murder?"

"Maybe he knew about it and threatened to expose them?" I added.

Realization dawned on her and she gasped, "Do you think so?"

"I don't know but I'll definitely need to meet with the copper-haired bridesmaid."

Wednesday morning was a picture-perfect morning and Harley and I spent just a few hours in the office with paperwork before heading out.

In addition to the maid of honor, Kelly Lyston, there were two other bridesmaids. Michelle Hopewell was a short, plump brunette with curly hair. I remembered her from the wedding because she seemed to be the only one who was upset at the reception. The copper haired bridesmaid Paris thought the groom was cheating with was Natalie Jordan.

Natalie was a waitress at a local restaurant. She wasn't home when we called so we decided to start out questioning Michelle.

Michelle Hopewell still lived at home with her parents. Apparently, they were at work when we arrived, because only

Michelle answered the door and invited us inside. The Hopewell's lived in a modest bungalow in a working-class neighborhood. The yard was small but well maintained. Inside, I chuckled as I noticed the furniture was covered with plastic slip covers. I'd spent my life in a house just like this. My mother didn't want her '*good furniture*' dirty, so she covered it in plastic. There were plastic runners that went from the front door, through the entire carpeted area of the house and plastic on the furniture. It always stuck to the back of your legs in the summer. The only time that plastic came off was for important company. I hated that plastic.

As we sat, I started the ball rolling. "Miss Hopewell, we have your statement from Saturday, but we're hoping you may have remembered something that will help shed some light on what happened."

Michelle sniffed, dabbed her eyes and shook her head no. However, I noticed her eyes kept drifting to Harley. He must have noticed too, because without a word, we shifted roles and Harley took the lead.

He asked questions while I walked around the room, admiring the knick knacks on the bookcases and walls, pretending not to listen.

"Sometimes things that seem insignificant can be very important. You were in the wedding party and might have seen something without realizing." Harley continued, with just the right amount of hope in his voice. Harley's southern drawl always became more pronounced as he turned up the charm.

Michelle sniffed again and dabbed at her eyes.

Harley gave her his handkerchief.

She smiled timidly before taking it and blowing her nose. She wiped her eyes, hiccupped and sniffed. "I'm sorry, I mean I barely knew him but it was so sad to die like that."

I have to admit these were the first tears I'd seen anyone shed for JP Rollins. I wondered if they were sincere. Maybe she was one of those sensitive types who cried at Hallmark commercials on television.

Harley continued to charm and compliment Michelle and before long she scooted closer to him and added, "Well you know I don't exactly remember a lot. It was so horrible I must have blanked most of it out of my mind."

I mentally translated that statement to mean she had been drinking like a fish and wasn't paying any attention to anything except the open bar.

"I totally understand. That happens quite often." Harley laid it on. "But, can you think of anyone who may have wanted to harm Mr. Rollins?"

Michelle sniffed, before adding reluctantly, "Well...he wasn't always the nicest man."

"Really?" Harley feigned surprise.

I hid a smile and explored the bookshelves as though my life depended on finding just the right knick knack.

"Oh No. He could be really difficult sometimes. I remember once when we were younger, some of us girls wanted to spend a weekend in Wisconsin skiing and he absolutely refused. He said he *KNEW* what we wanted and he wasn't going to put up with that type of behavior." Michelle managed to get that statement out before sniffing, but couldn't resist the urge for long.

"Wow. That must have been disappointing for all of you, especially Samantha," Harley sympathized.

"OH YES! She was *FURIOUS*! She said she'd get even with him." More sniffs.

"Really, and did she?" Harley leaned toward her and asked as though they were sharing a secret.

She sniffed. "I probably shouldn't be telling you this, but she told me later she did get even with him."

Harley leaned even closer. "What did she do?"

"She put a laxative in his food." Still more sniffs.

Harley grinned. Only I could tell it was strained. "Did he ever find out?"

"I don't think so, but if he did, she never mentioned it."

"Did she do things like that often?"

"Oh yeah. After she got started, well it just got easier and easier." Perhaps she finally realized what she was saying because she stopped abruptly. "But she didn't do anything serious. I

mean she would never do anything that was dangerous or…
nothing really bad."

"Of course not." Harley reassured and turned up the
southern accent and the charm.

But, Michelle must have realized she'd said too much
because try as he might, Harley wasn't able to get anything else
out of her.

"Well, Michelle you've really been helpful. I've enjoyed
talking to you."

Sniff. "Me too."

He handed her a card, "If you think of anything else no
matter how insignificant it might seem, feel free to call me."

We left her sniffing at the front door, watching us drive off.

He looked at me. "She's going to be sniffing and calling me
every day with trivial crap until we solve this murder."

I smiled. "Thanks for taking one for the team."

Harley looked as if he would have liked to strangle me, but
instead rolled his eyes and said nothing.

We tried Natalie's apartment once more and this time we
lucked out. She wasn't there but her neighbor, a small elderly
woman in her eighties was outside as we knocked.

"She's not home," She said.

"Do you know where she is?" I asked.

She looked us over as if we were there to steal the furniture,
so we pulled out our shields and showed them to her.

She looked at them as though she were converting them to
memory. "She's probably at work. Usually works a double-shift
on Wednesdays and Thursdays."

"Can you tell us where she works?" I asked.

"Silver Stone Bar and Grill."

We thanked her and got in our car and headed for
Silver Stone.

Silver Stone was a bar located near the area in St. Joe's
equivalent to the 'Red Light District.' Topless bars, adult book
stores and street walkers provided the commerce around South
Kentucky Avenue. When the liquor laws changed in St. Joe,
Silver Stones was in jeopardy of losing their license. In a half-

hearted effort to reduce vice, lower the crime rate, and appease the concerned citizens, the city council decided to limit the number of drinking establishments in the city. As is often the case, the owners of Silver Stone found a loop hole and declared they were a restaurant that served alcohol, not just a bar, so they were allowed to continue. The only difference was they opened earlier, offered a small selection of food, and now required the waitresses to wear tops for safety.

Silver Stone was dark and it took a few moments for our eyes to adjust to the darkness. My shoes stuck to the floor and I was almost afraid to touch anything. There were tables and booths surrounding a stage with a pole. I showed my shield to the bartended and asked for Natalie Jordan.

He stopped long enough to point at the stage and then continued working. Police at Silver Stone were a regular occurrence and rated barely a glance from the few men at the bar and less from the employees.

Feeling a tug on my sleeve, I turned around to see Harley was pointing at the featured performer who was our copper-haired bridesmaid. Natalie Jordan was young, top heavy and agile. One of the waitresses approached the bar to place an order and we took advantage of the opportunity. We showed our shields again and asked where we could go to wait for Natalie. She motioned for us to follow her and she led us back stage.

She led us to a door in the back and then turned and went back to work. The dressing room was small and there were three other women in various degrees of undress preparing for their turn on stage. Thankfully, we didn't have long to wait for Natalie to finish her routine.

"Hey, you're those cops from the wedding?" She stared at us as she sat down and removed her makeup.

I nodded. "We need to ask you some questions. Is there some place quiet we can go?" I stepped aside to make way for the next performer as she sidled past me wearing little more than a g-string and a long pair of pearls, and made her way to the stage.

"Sure, let me throw some clothes on."

About fifteen minutes later, we were all seated at a small coffee shop about a block away. When we were seated at the booth, Natalie asked if we were paying. After getting a nod, she promptly called over a waitress and ordered a tuna fish sandwich, fries and a coke. Harley and I both ordered coffee.

Natalie played with the sugar packets on the table when she finally turned to us and smiled and asked, "So what brings you two to this neighborhood?"

"We need to ask you a few questions?"

She leaned back and stared. "Okay. Fire away."

Harley took out his notebook.

I started the questioning, "How long have you known Samantha?"

"Since we were in high school. We used to skip out of History Class together."

"And how long have you known Todd?"

She hesitated just a split second and went back to the sugar packets. "Not very long, maybe a couple of months." She avoided eye contact and fidgeted.

It didn't take a trained investigator to know she was hiding something.

The waitress brought our drinks. We waited until she left before continuing. I decided to cut to the chase. "How long have you been fooling around with him?"

Having just taken a sip of her coke, Natalie nearly spit it out. Instead, she swallowed and it went down the wrong pipe, leading to a coughing fit.

Harley patted her on the back and she eventually regained control enough to speak. "What makes you think there's anything going on with me and Todd?"

I stretched the truth a bit by saying "Someone saw you."

Natalie looked like a deer caught in the headlights of a car. She leaned across the table. "Sam doesn't know does she?"

"I don't know." I shrugged.

"Oh man. I told Todd we needed to cool it for a while. But he thought it was fun to screw around at the wedding, especially with me wearing that white dress and all."

"So tell us about it." Harley added.

The waitress brought Natalie's food and she tore into it like someone who hadn't eaten in a few days. She talked between chews. "We met at Sam's house and there was just this… chemistry. You know?" She smiled. "We just had this attraction. Then, he showed up at Silver Stones one night. I told him it wasn't right, I mean Sam and I are friends. You know? But the more we tried to stop, the harder it was. Then it was sort of like….dangerous. You know. Like, we didn't want to get caught, but maybe we did. I don't know."

"So what happened on Saturday?" I asked.

She wolfed down most of her fries and half her sandwich before she continued. "We all went to the church and got dressed. I got dressed really fast and then Todd came and said he wanted to do it one last time before he was a married man. So, we found this room downstairs and well… we did. Then, I went back upstairs and helped Sam get dressed." She paused. Then she shrugged. "Then there was the wedding. Afterwards, at the reception, Todd wanted to do it again, you know, the first time as a married man. But, I didn't want to. I mean there were so many people coming and going and…I was afraid we'd get caught." She shrugged. "But, well, we did. That must have been when they saw us." The fact she was sleeping with her friend's husband didn't seem to have an impact on her conscience or her appetite as she scarfed down the rest of her sandwich and fries.

"Where did you go to…ah…be alone at the reception?" Harley asked.

"The room in the back. Where her uncle was killed."

Harley and I exchanged glances and then I asked, "When was this?"

"I don't know. We had to wait until Sam was busy. Todd took me back there. And we did it."

"Did anyone see you?"

"Well they must have or you wouldn't be asking me about it."

"I mean, did *you* see anyone?" I asked.

She shook her head and avoided eye contact. She played with the sugar packets and then shook her head again.

"How about dessert?" Harley asked.

She nodded and I got the waitress attention. We needed to keep her talking. Obviously, food was the key.

She ordered apple pie with ice cream.

"It'll be easier if you tell us the truth." For someone who was sneaking around with her best friend's husband, she wasn't a very good liar.

She sighed. "I think her uncle saw us. He was in the kitchen when we came out."

The waitress brought the pie and set the plate in front of Natalie.

We waited while she took a few bites before we continued.

"What did he say?" I asked.

"Who?" She ate the pie and ice cream in about four bites, then used her fork to scrape up every bit of ice cream.

"JP Rollins." I tried to keep my voice steady. "What did JP say when he saw you two coming out of the back room?"

She shrugged. "I don't know. I didn't talk to him. I just went back to the reception. Todd said he'd take care of it."

Harley and I exchanged glances and she looked from one of us to the other, "I'm sure he didn't kill him. Todd would never do anything like that."

"Was that part of the plan? You two kill JP Rollins and then Todd either divorces or kills Samantha and inherits the money leaving the two of you with a pile of cash?"

Natalie's face turned beet red as she banged her hand on the table and yelled, "NO. NO. We didn't kill anyone. There was no plan. And we would never hurt Sam."

"Sleeping with her husband isn't hurting her?" Harley asked quietly.

Natalie looked as if she'd been slapped. Her face which was so red a moment ago was suddenly white as a sheet as the blood drained away. Her lip quivered, and tears began to stream down her face. "I never meant to hurt her. She's my friend. We just couldn't help it." She sniffed and used her arm to wipe her face. I handed her a clean handkerchief and she just stared at it for a few minutes, while tears streamed down her face.

Gruffly, I added, "Look. We need the truth. If you know anything about the murder, you need to come clean now!" I didn't think Todd Stevens, who cheated on his wife less than an hour after he was married, merited tears and he definitely didn't deserve anyone's unfailing loyalty.

"We didn't have a plan. It just happened. I wasn't thinking about the money. I swear to God. I didn't kill him and I know Todd didn't either."

"Can you prove it?" Harley asked.

"Well no, but he just wouldn't."

I was frustrated with her and decided a trip to the precinct might scare her into telling us what she knew.

"We're going to need you to come down to the precinct and answer some questions and this time you need to tell us the truth."

"Oh My God."

Two hours later Natalie Jordan had told us all of the intimate details of her liaisons with Todd Stevens. She still contended there was no plot to murder JP Rollins and she hadn't been involved. The only detail she recalled from the reception was she remembered seeing JP Rollins doing shots in the main reception and in her mind that proved Todd had definitely *NOT* killed him. She couldn't say definitely what time she saw him last, but she was positive it was later, after Todd talked to him.

Adultery is still a crime in some states, but was repealed in 1976 in Indiana. I was disappointed. I would have liked to have arrested both of them, even if it was only for adultery. Unfortunately, we had to let her go. A trip to the District Attorney's office dashed my hopes of getting a wire tap. He didn't feel we had enough evidence. I felt confident she would be getting in touch with Todd sooner or later. But maybe it would wait until he returned from his honeymoon.

The rest of the day we completed paperwork on this case and the mountain of other cases we were both working on simultaneously. By the end of the day, I was physically tired, but mentally excited about the second day of my class.

I was amazed to find there were even more people in class tonight than on Monday. At break, I learned the original students from Monday had spread the word to their friends and that was the cause for the increased numbers. I wasn't sure if I should be flattered or not. As I explained to Paris when I called her after class, my ego would love to believe they heard what an excellent teacher I was, and that was why so many more students suddenly enrolled in my class. However, I remembered my college days and more than likely I had been deemed an easy mark. Like sharks in a pool of blood, the students might just be circling in on the new professor. They would attack when my defenses were down.

When Paris finished laughing, she reminded me I was licensed to carry a gun. Not a sign of an easy mark.

Despite my trepidation, the second night went even better than the first. They had a ton of questions and just as on the first night, most of them spent their one and only break firing questions at me. Maybe I was more of a ham than I realized because I had to admit I found the attention flattering. The truly stimulating thing was that their questions were insightful and delved in to the depths of the criminal justice system. We talked about evidence and procedures and they particularly loved the real case examples Judge Browning had encouraged me to include in the curriculum. They surprised me by applauding when I told them I had gotten approval for them to participate on a ride along and also to take a tour of the station. St. Joe wasn't exactly a hot bed of crime and vice. Many of these individuals were from large cities like Chicago and New York; but most of them had formed their opinions about criminals, and the police for that matter, by watching CSI or Law and Order on television. I was afraid they would feel like a field trip was too juvenile. But Judge Browning reassured me; and as is often the case, he was right. St. Joe was a good place to get your feet wet. Again, I left feeling rejuvenated and excited. But I didn't have nearly as difficult a time falling asleep. I found myself sorting through all of the evidence we'd acquired on the murder of JP Rollins. I wondered if Samantha knew her husband was cheating on her with her oldest friend. Did she know her mother was JP Rollins' wife? She had to know her father was his brother but was that the extent of her knowledge? There was only one way we were going to get the answer to these questions. We'd have to go to the source.

CHAPTER 10

line and was thoroughly confused about her friend. Did she know her mother was JP Rollins' lover? She had to know but either was his mark or but was that the extent of her knowledge? There was only one way we were going to get the answer to these questions. We'd have to go to the source.

Thursday morning Harley and I were seated in Chief Mike's office trying to convince him we needed to fly to Florida to talk to the honeymooners. Unfortunately, hard economic times and a tight budget were working against us. Normally, working on a high profile murder loosened the purse strings. Unfortunately, it seemed JP Rollins was universally disliked from City Hall to local news stations. After the initial day of reporters and television cameras, his murder barely rated a mention in the local papers. Chief Mike and the mayor participated in a joint press conference immediately following the news of the murder, but JP Rollins' murder wasn't selling papers.

"Come on, Chief. How are we supposed to solve this without talking to the two top suspects." Harley resorted to something close to a whine at the prospect of a trip to Florida and Disney World.

"You will solve it by following the evidence and locating the murderer. They'll be back in two days. The Florida police are keeping an eye out to make sure they don't high tail it out of the country. But, that's the best I can do for you."

I listened to Harley and Chief Mike debate back and forth for a bit and then decided to surrender. "Okay Chief, I get it, no trip to Florida. But, at least can we get our wire tap?" I still felt Natalie and Todd would be in touch. If she was going to warn him we'd be asking questions, I'd like to know first.

"Not up to me. You'll have to find some more evidence and take it back to the District Attorney."

"I know but he respects you. He might just bend a bit if you were to have a word with him." I said.

Chief Mike liked to have his ego stroked the same as the rest of us. He sat back in his chair and looked at me as if he was trying to figure out what I was up to. I looked him in the eyes as innocent as a newborn babe.

"Okay, but you darned well better get something more than lovers making kiss-kiss over the phone."

I was happy with that and Harley and I left to see to the details. I just hoped it wasn't too late. I was hopeful she hadn't called or sent him a message which might put him on guard.

Chief Mike was as good as his word and a few short hours later, we had our wire tap in place. Hopefully, it would yield rewards.

"Now what?" Harley asked, as we sorted through paperwork.

"I still think we need to look at the first rule of homicide."

"Motive?"

"Exactly. Who benefits from the death of JP Rollins?"

"We know that. The daughter—ultimately," Harley said.

An idea had been forming since last night's lecture that I wanted to pursue. In talking to the law students about motive and police procedure, I stressed the importance of motive and following the evidence. Let's face it; unless the killer is a psychopath, there was usually a reason to kill. Whether it was jealously, revenge, greed, love or hate; people killed because there was some profit in it for them—they got something out of it.

"Why now? She's had years to do him in if she wanted to. Why wait until now?" I asked aloud.

"Maybe it's the husband then. Maybe he thought he was marrying a rich girl and would be on easy street."

"He'd have to be a fool to believe JP Rollins would just turn over his fortune like that."

"Agreed, but, look at what we know about him up to this point. His actions don't exactly scream rocket scientist."

"He may not be very bright. But, it takes a lot of guts or anger or desperation to drive a knife through someone's chest and given the condition he was in at the reception, I just don't know if he could have done it; at least not without help."

"So, what are you thinking?" Harley asked.

"There has to be a motive. Someone benefited from this death one way or another. There has to be some reason to risk everything."

"Do you mean financially?" Harley pondered, sitting up straight in his chair as he looked at me.

"Well, JP Rollins was a billionaire. People have killed for a lot less reasons. He was mean and hated by a lot of people for many years, so why kill him now?"

Harley paused for almost a minute before adding, "You think the wedding changed something."

"Yeah. Ultimately Samantha benefits, but not immediately. I think we need to look a little more closely at the business." Standing up, I put my jacket on and grabbed my keys.

"So where are we going?" Harley added as he grabbed his jacket and followed me down the hall.

"To get a copy of the will and talk to the trustees. I think we need to ask some different questions."

Richard Stout was out when we arrived at his office, but his clerk got us a copy of JP Rollins's will; which was helpful. So, we decided to visit the other trustees.

I'd met Henrietta Thomas, a few months ago when I was investigating a money laundering case. Ms. Thomas was the president of First State Bank. Sharp as a tack, mid-forties, Ms. Thomas was not only the president of First State Bank, but the first female bank president in St. Joe history. She would never win a beauty pageant, but I would bank on her intellect in virtually any competition she entered, no pun intended. She was a good judge of character and a shrewd business woman. I was definitely interested in hearing her opinions of JP Rollins.

Without an appointment, we lucked out. Having just arrived from a banking convention, Ms. Thomas had stopped in the office to drop off a few documents and catch up on her email and paperwork. As we entered her office, she smiled and I noticed she looked slightly less formal than normal. Wearing a pair of slacks and a blouse rather than her usual suit, this was probably as casual as bank presidents got.

"It's nice to see you again detectives. I hope you don't have any other money laundering cases." She indicated we should sit in the chairs in front of her large desk.

We sat. "Not this time. Although I don't know if I ever thanked you properly for all of your help and that of your staff; it was invaluable in wrapping everything up," I said with sincerity.

"You did, but I'm glad we were able to help. Now, what can I do for you?" She sat, quietly and waited.

Harley had his notebook out.

He'd met Ms. Thomas previously, but for some reason he never particularly cared for her. He said she reminded him of a teacher he had in elementary school; apparently, the memory wasn't a pleasant one. He rarely spoke in her presence, so I knew I'd have to get the ball rolling. "I know you've been away at a conference, but I assume you heard of the death of JP Rollins." I watched her face, but saw no signs of fear or relief.

"I did. I didn't know you were investigating?"

"We heard you were one of the trustees handling his estate. How well acquainted were you?"

With a sigh she added, "My relationship with JP Rollins was purely business. We sat on several boards together. He's banked with First State for many years...I..." she stopped, thought a moment and then started again. "I've known JP Rollins for many years. We haven't always agreed. In fact we disagreed on most issues." She seemed to relax a bit. "We had some real battles. JP was not what I would call a kind man. He had moments when he could be a gentleman...but they were too few and far between." She shook her head. "Most of the time he was demanding and arrogant and extremely controlling. He didn't believe in compromise and expected 150 percent dedication and loyalty from everyone, even his banker." She smiled at this.

"Did you know the terms of his will?" I asked aloud.

"Oh yes. He told me."

"When was this?"

She thought for a moment then added, "About a month ago. Right after he found out his daughter was getting married. He told me he intended to change his will to make sure '*that young fool didn't get a dime of his money*.'" Ms Thomas mimicked Rollins puffed up, and condescending mannerisms.

Harley mustered up the courage to speak. "You mean he changed his will after his daughter announced she was getting married?" His voice sounded almost normal, even to my ears. I'm sure Ms. Thomas didn't notice it was slightly higher pitched than normal.

She nodded.

"Do you by chance know what the provisions of the will were before this?" I asked.

Shaking her head, "Sorry, but like I said, we weren't exactly what you might call *best buds*."

"If you two weren't that close, then why did he pick you for trustee over his account?" Harley asked, and his voice really was normal this time. I guess he'd gotten over his old school teacher.

"You know I wondered the same thing. I would like to think that even though we seldom agreed, he still respected me."

"But?" I wondered out loud.

"But, I doubt it." She sighed. "I suppose it was because he knew I was familiar with his accounts. But who knows with JP." She shrugged.

"Do you know anyone who wanted to kill Mr. Rollins?" I should have been accustomed to the people who knew JP Rollins laughing at that question; but I wasn't. I definitely wasn't expecting that response from Henrietta Thomas, but that's what I got. Ms. Thomas was always so straight laced and proper I didn't even know she knew how to laugh, but she revealed an unusual sense of humor.

We waited until she pulled herself together; which didn't take long. But, even then she found it hard to keep a smile off her face.

"I'm so sorry. I know murder is nothing to laugh at. But, well, your question just struck me as funny. Based on what I know of JP Rollins, I think you would be hard pressed to find anyone who didn't want to murder him at one time or another. He could be incredibly difficult and made a large number of enemies."

"Any one person in particular?" I tried again.

She paused a moment and then added, "Well, honestly it's hard to imagine. I mean murder is so violent. But, JP could be extremely difficult. I remember a few years ago, he wanted to buy a horse. But the owner didn't want to sell. JP got so angry he ended up buying the mortgage on the farm, all the hay within a two hundred mile radius and every business the owner came into contact with. He made it virtually impossible for that poor man and his family to walk out of their front door without encountering JP Rollins. They eventually sold the horse to him." She shook her head sadly, "And, for a lot less than it was worth just to be free of JP Rollins. I was there when the guy signed the papers, he was furious."

"Furious enough to kill?" Harley asked.

"Maybe. But that was a long time ago. I just mentioned it as an example. There were probably hundreds of similar stories. JP was a man who never took no for an answer. He was determined to get his way, no matter who he had to roll over to do it."

"Well someone finally managed to get the point across." I commented, again no pun intended.

CHAPTER 11

After leaving First State Bank, we decided to check out the third and final trustee, Frank Logan, VP of Operations for JP Rollins Enterprises.

JP Rollins Enterprises may have been a multi-billion dollar company but you would never have guessed it by looking at the offices. The few executives Rollins employed were not your white collar, blue suited Harvard Business School graduates. Instead, JP Rollins believed in promoting internally. Frank Logan looked more like a linebacker for the Pittsburgh Steelers back during the days of the *Steel Curtain* with Mean Joe Green, than an executive at a corporation. Harley and I weren't what anyone would categorize as light weights. Harley was six foot one, and I've got another two inches on him. Frank Logan had about 5 more inches on me. I'd guess his weight was in the 300's but like professional athletes like, Shaquille O'Neal, at least in his early days, Logan was all muscle. He had a grip like a vice which forced me to hide a wince, while Harley shook his hand and flexed his fingers several times to get the blood circulating again.

"I'm sorry," he said sincerely noticing Harley still flexing his fingers. He directed us to chairs in the tiny cramped space he called an office, located on the floor of the trucking factory.

"Don't worry about it." Harley flexed. "Thankfully I'm a lefty."

Logan frowned. "I forget my own strength sometimes, sorry."

I sat in the one guest chair in the office, while Logan rolled in another chair he'd drummed up somewhere for Harley before squeezing himself behind his desk.

"What can I do for you gentleman?" He asked, enthusiastically.

I couldn't tell if Frank Logan was excited because he was anxious to talk to us, or because he didn't get a lot of visitors. That's not a reception that homicide detectives get very often. It threw us both off for a moment. As cops, we were more accustomed to reluctance and dread than welcoming excitement, but Logan seemed genuine, if the sparkle in his eyes was any indication.

"We're investigating the murder of JP Rollins. We would like to ask a few questions." I jumped in.

Logan leaned across the desk and looked as though he'd like nothing better than to answer our questions. "Sure. Definitely. I don't know how much I can help you, but I'll sure try."

"How long have you worked for JP Rollins Enterprises?" Harley took out his notepad and pencil. I noticed he was flexing his hand less frequently now. Perhaps the circulation had returned.

"I started not long after graduating from MAC-U. I was an intern while at university on a football scholarship."

"Really? Football. Who would have guessed." Harley managed to look sincere and there was barely a twinge of the sarcasm I knew was behind the words.

"Oh yes. I was an All-American. I was a second-round draft pick for the Colts." The pride was definitely there behind his words and in his eyes.

"So, what happened?" Harley asked aloud.

"Blew out my knee at training camp – ended my career." Logan wasn't over that lost opportunity. He opened his desk drawer and pulled out a picture which he passed across to me.

It was a picture of Frank Logan, a little younger, but not much lighter, with his Colts jersey and Tony Dungy shaking hands. He looked like a kid with a huge grin on his face.

"Wow! That's a tough break." I handed the photo to Harley.

"Yeah, but I guess it just wasn't meant to be." He almost sounded convinced, but not quite.

"So, you came to work here immediately after the NFL?" I asked.

He nodded. "I'd worked for Mr. Rollins as a part of my internship during school, so I was thrilled he wanted me, but he was a big football fan and supported the university."

"He must have really liked you a lot to make you VP of Operations." Harley added.

He shook his head. "I didn't start out as Vice President of Operations. I had to work my way up." He smiled, but for the first time since we entered, that smile didn't make it to his eyes. He paused briefly, then shook it off and continued. "I started out doing a bit of everything. I've done just about everything from driving trucks to loading, inventory, everything. I wanted to learn as much about the business as I could. I think Mr. Rollins liked that."

"So, how long have you worked here?" I asked. He looked too young to have been working that long.

"About ten years now." He certainly looked a lot younger than he was. I wouldn't have guessed him out of his twenties.

"So you worked your way up to VP of Operations in just ten years? That's amazing. You must be a real quick learner." Harley added.

His eyes flashed and I could see a muscle on his jaw tense. "Just because I was a jock doesn't mean I'm stupid. Not all jocks are dumb." Logan had a sore spot and Harley had found it.

"I'm sorry. I didn't mean to imply you were." Harley held up his hands as he apologized.

"I know I don't look like I'm much more than a jock. But, I do have brains. I graduated with a 3.2 GPA with a business degree from one of the best business schools in the country." Logan said huffily.

"I'm sorry. Really." Harley looked sincere.

Logan glared at Harley for another few seconds then he flipped a switch mentally. He smiled broadly. "Apology accepted." He reached across the desk and smacked Harley on the shoulder in a good natured manner. "I never could hold a grudge. It just bites my butt that people think I'm stupid. Players used to make that mistake on the field. But, they'd learn soon enough," he chuckled in remembrance."

"I'll bet they did." Harley winced and shifted his shoulder in an effort to stretch from the friendly smack.

"People made the mistake of underestimating me. I always made sure they paid for that."

"Sounds like JP Rollins didn't underestimate you." I said casually.

"I think he did at first. He only gave me grunt work jobs. Any Joe off the street could have done the mindless work he gave me at first. But, I showed him I wasn't just a hard worker, but I also had a brain." He tapped the side of his head. "I showed him I was smart. I knew my stuff."

"Sounds like you and JP got along well together." I said offhandedly.

Logan seemed to hold back for the first time since we'd entered the room. "I suppose so. We got along pretty well. I came in, did my work and that's it. We weren't best friends or anything. But, work is work."

"He must have trusted you. He named you as trustee over his estate." Harley said, with just a slight amount of awe in his voice.

"I suppose he did trust me." He sat taller. "I earned his trust."

"That's saying something right there." I added.

He nodded. "JP could be pretty demanding sometimes. He expected dedication. As long as you did what he wanted, you were fine. One thing you learn playing on a team is how to play well with others."

It wasn't just the words he said, but something more behind them. I started thinking that perhaps our athletic friend had more going on than that friendly demeanor. Maybe there was more to this guy than originally met the eye. No matter how much of a sports fan JP Rollins may have been, he was certainly no fool. He would never have turned control of his business over to someone who was incompetent. If that were the case, he could have just allowed his daughter/niece to inherit the funds without setting up a trust. No, JP Rollins must have seen something in this gentle giant.

"You weren't at the wedding." Harley stated this as a fact rather than a question.

"No." Logan paused before adding, "Like I said, we worked together. We weren't exactly best friends. We didn't socialize outside of work. I was invited, but...I had other plans"

For such a successful businessman, he was a remarkably poor liar.

"May I ask where you were?" I asked as politely as I could.

"Sure. I was at the football game. I have season tickets. I never miss a home game."

"We were at the game too." Harley added conspiratorially, as if it was a huge secret. "At least for the first half anyway."

A light went on in Logan's eyes as he leaned forward excitedly to add, "Wasn't that a great game. I mean that pass in the fourth quarter was incredible. It was third down and nineteen and we had the ball on our own four yard line, when Zaq rolls right and throws the ball fifty yards down field, Morrison leaps in the air and comes down with the pass. Then, he was off." At this point, Logan stood up and reached into the air, grabbed an imaginary ball and then posed for an instant before faking and dodging as he continued, "He tucked that puppy under his arm and all anyone saw was the back of his jersey and a lot of dust as he raced for the end zone." Logan spiked his imaginary ball and did a victory dance before flinging himself back into his seat.

I don't know if Harley was more stunned by the agility Logan demonstrated as he maneuvered around the cramped desk to relive the glory moments of the game, or by the fact that we'd missed an incredible game.

We asked a few other questions, but it was clear, there wasn't anything else he could tell us. He hadn't been at the wedding or the reception.

Afterward, Harley and I discussed Henrietta Thomas and Frank Logan with Chief Mike.

"I don't think he was lying about being at the football game." Harley said bopping around the room like a mime.

"But you think he was lying about something?" Chief Mike choked out in between chuckles.

I nodded. "He said he was invited to the wedding, but didn't go because of the game. At first I thought he was lying about the game, but he obviously wasn't lying about that. So, he must have lied about being invited."

"Why? It eliminates him as a murder suspect." Chief Mike was always one for the obvious.

"True, but maybe he felt like someone in his position should have been invited." That sounded weak even to my ears.

"Why would it matter now?" Harley asked.

I shook my head. "No idea. We have a copy of the people who signed the guest book at the church. We don't have a copy of the people who received invitations."

"Do you think we need one?" Harley was about as eager as I was to find something that would end this case.

I shrugged. "I don't know. But, at least we can check whether or not Frank Logan was invited."

"What about the other trustees?" Chief Mike leaned back in his chair and squinted at me over the top of his glasses. He hated going to doctors, including optometrist. His prescription was about twenty years old, and it was clear it was no longer effective, as he often had to remove his glasses to read. The force required regular physicals and target practice. I have no idea how Chief Mike had managed around the rules, but it was clear he wasn't keeping up with his appointments.

Harley flipped through his notes before answering. "Henrietta Thomas was away at a banking convention." He flipped. "Richard Stout claimed to have attended the wedding ceremony at the church but had other plans and left afterward, skipping the reception."

"Why?" Chief Mike looked puzzled. Taking his glasses off, he twirled them around before adding, "Most people go to the reception and skip the formal ceremony."

"Especially when there's an open bar" Harley added.

"Exactly," Chief Mike leaned forward. He was on to something, what it was, I wasn't sure. "Why did he skip the reception? That's a bit too convenient. Check out his alibi." Chief Mike leaned back as if he'd solved the case.

I wasn't sure he had, but he had a point and we needed to follow up with the lawyer anyway.

We weren't able to track down Richard Stout the remainder of the day and no one at the law firm could confirm his whereabouts for the previous Saturday. We'd have to dig a little to figure that out.

The remainder of our day was spent with paperwork, paperwork and more paperwork. Most people think a policeman's life was exciting car chases, gun fights and locking up bad guys. The reality was that most of my life was spent doing paperwork. Failure to document everything could mean the difference between jail time and acquittal when a case finally made it to court.

When I'd had my fill of paperwork, I left. I stopped by Mama B's on my way home that evening. She was sitting in her recliner with the door open watching reruns of the *Andy Griffith*.

I knocked before opening the door, which I knew was already open.

"You know you shouldn't keep your front door open, anybody can just walk in." I said reproachfully as I came in and planted a kiss on her cheek.

She smiled as she always did, as if I was slightly touched in the head and kept on rocking, "Take a load off. You look tired."

"Thanks. It's good to see you too." I don't know why I bothered being sarcastic, because it was wasted on her. She just kept on rocking and watching *Andy Griffith*.

"I got some chicken and noodles in the kitchen. Go and fix yourself a plate." She waved me toward the kitchen.

She would never be able to accept the fact I wouldn't starve if she didn't feed me every time she saw me. Of course, I didn't feel too motivated to try to convince her. The smell of the chicken and noodles was amazing and my stomach growled.

"Harley loves your chicken and noodles. He'll be angry when he finds out you cooked it and I didn't bring him with me." I stood up and headed for the kitchen.

"I put a bowl in the fridge for you to take for him." Mama B yelled from the living room. "And you make sure you bring my Tupperware container back when he's done."

I smiled to myself as I opened the refrigerator and saw she had loaded two large containers full of chicken and noodles. Sitting on top of the chicken and noodles was another smaller container which contained cornbread mix. I smiled to myself realizing she realized the cornbread would taste better fresh and had mixed it for him so all he'd have to do would be to bake it to enjoy with his chicken and noodles. She'd thought of everything.

Returning to the living room with my plate of chicken and noodles and corn bread, I ate a few spoonfuls before saying, "I should have my feelings hurt. You used to just fix containers for me to take home and now you're fixing them for my partner. I think his bowl is even bigger than mine. If I didn't know better, I might think you didn't love me anymore."

Mama B smiled and shrugged before adding, "You got Paris to cook for you now. I don't have to worry 'bout you eating. Harley ain't got nobody to look after him." Mama B's body shook as she silently laughed at me.

She was ecstatic Paris and I were dating. Although she never married herself, she wouldn't be satisfied until I and everyone around her were happily married off with children. "So now you've managed to bring Paris and me together are you about to start working on Harley?" I laughed. "I better tell him to run."

"You can run, but you can't hide." She laughed. "Besides, it ain't natural for men and women to be single. That's why the good Lord created men *AND* women. But I ain't got to worry 'bout Harley no mo.'" Mama B added.

"Why not?"

"That's your job?"

I just about choked on my food. "*WHAT*? Why would I do that? Harley is perfectly happy and content as a bachelor. Unlike someone else I know, I don't believe in getting involved in other people's personal lives."

Mama B, sniffed and continued to rock. "You know they say you can lead a horse to water but you can't make him drink. But that ain't true. If you want to make a horse drink, all you gotta do is show him another horse that's drinking. It won't be long before that other horse will realize how thirsty he really is. Before you know it, he's drinking right along with the other horses."

I was speechless. I stared at her for a full minute. Then, I burst out laughing. I laughed all the way home and each time I looked at Harley's chicken and noodles or thought about him, I chuckled. He was going to have to drink whether he liked it or not and apparently, I was the horse that was going to drive him to the river.

CHAPTER 12

Friday Harley and I had two major objectives, tracking down Richard Stout and confirming Frank Logan's alibi. Both items eluded us. Richard Stout's office was closed, as was indicated by a sign left on the door and the answering service, but would reopen on Monday.

Frank Logan, or someone using his season ticket, entered the game on the Saturday of the murder. But entering the stadium doesn't guarantee he stayed for the entire game. We wasted half the day trying to track down the owners of the seats next to Frank Logan's only to discover they were purchased by a scalper who admitted selling the tickets. The only description he could offer up was the buyer had plenty of cash. Great.

MAC-U, like most college campuses had a student union where the masses went for everything from hamburgers to sweatshirts. But, MAC-U also had a really good, four star restaurant in the campus inn. We decided to replenish our energy by grabbing a bite to eat there. The food was good, the service was fantastic and surprisingly enough the prices weren't bad, either. Plus, as a member of faculty, I got a discount, all really good reasons for us to give it a try.

"This is really good." Harley used his French dip sandwich to sop up the last of the au jus before shoveling it into his mouth.

I nodded. "One of my students told me about it."

"You get a discount too? That's awesome. Discounted football tickets, discounted meals, you're going to clean up just for teaching a few classes."

"You can join me. I'm sure they could use additional faculty."

"Ha! Not likely. Nice try." Harley finished his sandwich and glanced at the desert tray that was located just a little too close to our seats. "You know, I think we're going about this all wrong"

I must have looked as puzzled as I felt, because Harley laughed and then added, "Trying to verify Frank Logan's attendance at the football game is like finding a beautiful woman at a beauty pageant."

"Okay."

"Maybe we should verify where he wasn't rather than verify where he was."

"You mean instead of trying to confirm his alibi, let's just verify that he wasn't anywhere near the wedding or the reception?"

"It may be the only way. I mean, let's face it. There were close to eighty thousand people at that game. He could have come and gone about a hundred times and we wouldn't be able to prove that he didn't just go to the rest room."

"Good point. It certainly isn't the ideal situation, but it beats running around in circles."

With a new plan of attack, Harley and I set out to find someone who could attest to seeing Frank Logan near the crime scene or who would validate that he wasn't. Hours later, we were just about at the same place. No one could swear they saw him but most were too inebriated to remember who was there. Most eye witnesses weren't very reliable immediately following a crime. The more time that passed, the less likely they were to recall the little details that police relied on, but seemed totally irrelevant normally. The trail felt pretty cold. Little did we know things were already heating up.

CHAPTER 13

When we returned to the station, all hell had broken loose. As soon as we stepped into the precinct, I was handed at least ten telephone messages and was told Chief Mike and the District Attorney were waiting for us. That's never a good sign. The messages would have to wait. So, I shoved them into my pocket and Harley and I hurried to the D.A.'s office.

As soon as we arrived, we were waved in by the secretary and were immediately greeted by Chief Mike, the District Attorney and the Assistant District Attorney. The DA was a grey-haired man in his late fifties who looked more like a mob boss than an attorney. However, his reputation for being tough on crime had gotten him elected and re-elected when every other member of his political party had been summarily dismissed from office a few years back. Indiana had always been a very conservative state but Robert Martinelli was a Democrat that defied political labels. He had earned a reputation for doing the right thing, even if that meant turning in a member of his own family. I knew Chief Mike and Rob Martinelli had become friends many years ago. While most people in Martinelli's position were at the country club playing golf and sipping martini's, Martinelli preferred drinking beer and bowling at the local bowling alley. Rumor had it Martinelli was a pretty good bowler, almost professional caliber. He was reported to have bowled over fifteen perfect games, earning him a measure of fame and recognition few, at least in St. Joe, ever came close to achieving.

Martinelli's office had old, leather furniture, selected for comfort rather than looks. Upon entering, Martinelli motioned for us to sit.

"It's about time. What took you two so long?" Chief Mike asked the moment we were seated.

"Sorry sir. We were verifying alibis. What's up?" I knew something big must have happened for Chief Mike to be so excited.

"We've had some developments," Martinelli said.

"So the wire tap worked? What did you get? Did he confess?" Harley asked excitedly.

"Not exactly." Martinelli pointed toward the silent figure in the corner. "Perhaps Tim can fill you in." Tim Austen was a thirty-something, Assistant District Attorney. Austen was the only child of two of St. Joe's elite and was destined for greatness from the time he took his first steps. His father was the Chief of Surgery at the local hospital while his mother was a socialite who sat on the boards of almost every charity in the state. Tim's grandfather had been mayor and governor of the state about twenty years ago and the family was said to be able to trace their roots back to the Mayflower. But, Austen was no light-weight. Graduating first in his class from MAC-U, Tim Austen was as smart as he was connected. His future appeared to be solid. The truly remarkable thing was I liked him. He had always been fair in all the dealings I'd had with him. Besides, he had a fairly decently jump shot that helped the law enforcement team take down the Fire Chief and Fire Safety's basketball team a few months ago in the Mayor's summer recreational fundraiser. He also had a good sense of humor.

"What's going on?" I asked, as Tim approached the table.

"Well, you were right about the girl, Natalie Jordan and Todd Stevens. They were definitely fooling around. She sent him a series of text messages." Tim held up a document which I knew at once to be a transcript of the phone messages.

"Anything interesting?" Harley glanced over my shoulder as I browsed through the transcript.

A quick glance through the transcription of text messages showed just about what you would expect. Natalie Jordan told Todd we were aware of their affair. Todd reassured Natalie there was nothing to worry about, and finally, the type of intimate messages I was always amazed people still did in light of twenty-first century technology and the recent celebrity exposés that had caused problems not only in this country, but in others.

It was salacious, but certainly hadn't warranted a visit from the District Attorney. Puzzled, I dropped the transcript on the desk. "So what's the real issue? We knew they were screwing around. That certainly isn't anything to warrant this type of…attention."

Martinelli smiled. "You're right. The text messages were apparently the catalyst for the explosion that followed."

"Explosion?" Harley looked puzzled, and then the light bulb went off and you could see in it in his eyes. "You mean Samantha saw those messages?"

Each person nodded and I settled back trying to think what the implications were from that.

"So what happened?" Harley asked excitedly.

Martinelli nodded at Tim to do the honors, and he filled us in. "We don't really know everything. Best we can tell, Samantha saw the text messages and confronted Todd. A big fight ensued. She threw everything she could at him— literally. The hotel estimates the damages to be somewhere in the range of thirty thousand dollars.

Harley whistled and added, "Wow! That's a lot of money. What did she hit him with?"

Tim smiled. "What didn't she hit him with would be easier. She broke the television, the windows, and every mirror." He handed pictures.

"I've seen less damage from hurricanes," I shook my head in disbelief.

"The police were called, but before they could arrive, she did a bunk."

I sat up straight. "Are you telling me she got away?"

Tim nodded.

"You have got to be kidding me?" Harley was as shocked as I was.

"I thought the Florida authorities were alerted not to allow them to leave?" I asked incredulous she had managed to slip through the cracks like that.

Chief Mike looked like he was about ready to choke, "They swear she didn't fly out on a commercial flight. She may have rented a car, but I doubt it. She must be around there somewhere."

At that moment, the phone rang and Martinelli picked up. After a few seconds, he instructed the caller to show them in. He returned the phone to the cradle. "Gentlemen, I think we are about to gain some insight into what happened to Mrs. Stevens."

At that moment, the door opened, and in walked Richard Stout. Red eyed, and haggard, he looked as though he hadn't slept in a couple of days. His clothes were wrinkled and smelled of smoke and alcohol. Richard Stout had aged considerably in the few days since we'd last seen him. He entered the room tentatively. Introductions were made and he sat down.

"I'm sure you've all heard Samantha Rollins..ah, Stevens, has disappeared from Florida." Stout added.

"Do you know where she is?" Tim Austen asked.

Stout looked pained, but nodded. "Yes. I do."

We waited, but Stout simply pinched his nose and sat in silence.

"Well, are you going to tell us? Your client is involved in a murder investigation. She was cleared to go on her honeymoon but was told not to go anywhere else. You realize this changes everything." Chief Mike threw the questions like a rock at Stout who took the hit.

"Last night I got a call." Stout started.

"From Mrs. Stevens?" Chief Mike interrupted.

"No. From Frank Logan. And, if you gentleman will please let me talk without interruption, I will tell you everything. That's why I'm here." He rubbed the back of his neck. "I have a splitting headache. Can I trouble you for a couple of aspirin and a glass of water?"

Martinelli pulled open a drawer and pulled out a bottle of aspirin and handed them to Stout. There was a small fridge behind his chair and he swiveled around and opened it and took out a bottle of water and handed it to him.

Stout opened the aspirin and poured at least four into his palm, then chucked them to the back of his throat. We waited while he unscrewed the water and took a swig to wash down the pills.

We waited quietly.

When he finished he took a deep breath. "Thank you. As I was saying, Last night I got a call from Frank Logan. He had received a call from Samantha."

"What? How come we don't have this on the record?" Chief Mike was unable to contain his surprise.

"Because the trace was just on her husband's phone, not hers," Tim said.

"Please go on Mr. Stout." Martinelli added.

"She called Frank Logan hysterical. She'd discovered her husband was having an affair with one of her friends." He shook his head. "But you already know that."

We nodded.

"Good. What you may not know, I have to admit I didn't know this either, was that Samantha and Frank Logan had been…involved for many months before she met Todd Stevens."

"What!" We all shouted in unison.

"Are you kidding me?" Chief Mike was beside himself. He paced back and forth and mumbled under his breath. Fortunately, the district attorney's office was larger and allowed more room for pacing.

"I had no idea myself until I got the call from Logan. He and Samantha kept it very quiet. I think for her it may have been a way of getting back at JP."

"That's interesting but so far, not a crime. Why keep it silent?" I asked.

Stout smiled timidly. "You'd have to have known JP Rollins to fully understand." He shook his head. "I guess Logan wanted to tell JP about him and Samantha, but she was adamantly against it. Ultimately, she ended the relationship about two months ago."

"Wait. Wasn't she engaged to Todd Stevens three months ago?" Harley asked incredulous.

Stout nodded. He looked as though he'd been through the ringer, blood shot eyes, and he kept rubbing his temple, obviously the aspirin hadn't kicked in yet.

"Would you care for a cup of coffee?" Martinelli asked as a mere formality, as he had clearly already decided Stout needed coffee and had risen and walked to a credenza on the other side of the room, where a coffee pot and mugs were laid out. Martinelli poured a cup of coffee and brought it to Stout who accepted it gratefully.

You almost, wouldn't have noticed the shaking in his hands as he drank the strong coffee. After a few sips, he seemed more in control and placed the cup on the edge of the desk.

"I believe the relationship was off and on again several times in the past few months. I think initially, Samantha thought hanging out with Todd would throw JP off the scent and give him something else to focus his attention."

"Why did Frank Logan tell you all of this now?" I asked, while Stout took another sip of coffee.

"Because last night she called him and told him she had made a mistake in marrying Todd. She told him she wanted a divorce and… she told him she was pregnant with his baby."

"*WHAT!*" The Chief shouted.

I think Martinelli was shocked too although he hid it well. Only a small twitch at the corners of his mouth gave away his feelings.

Harley had yet to master the poker face and was staring open mouthed. "We should arrest her." Harley seemed angrier than I'd ever seen him.

I stared at him and wondered where the anger came from.

After a few deep breaths, he explained, "I can't believe any woman would consume alcohol when she knows she's pregnant. She should be locked up."

Stout shrugged. "I don't know how long she's known about the baby." Stout added. "But Logan only found out last night. As VP of Operations, he is entitled to certain…privileges."

The look on our faces must have been hilarious because Stout laughed before clarifying, "Not those types of privileges.

I mean corporate privileges. Logan has access to the Rollins enterprises corporate jet. A few years ago, JP bought into a private jet co-op. It allows businessmen to share the ownership and maintenance of a private jet."

We must have all looked incredulous, but Stout continued, "Logan was able to get the jet late last night. He flew to Orlando and met Samantha. They then flew to Reno."

"RENO?" Chief Mike stopped pacing long enough to shout the one word, and then resumed pacing. "Are you serious? She left Disney World for Reno?"

"Reno only has a six-week residency requirement for getting a divorce," Tim volunteered. Stout nodded and sipped his coffee.

"Divorced? Are you kidding? She has been married less than one week. You're telling me she left her honeymoon in freakin' Disney World to fly to Reno for a divorce?" Chief Mike was practically sputtering as he paced.

"Yes. That's what I'm saying." Stout added as calm as a man in the hot seat could be.

"Let me get this straight. When she called, Frank Logan took the Rollins corporate jet and flew to Disney World to get her and then had flown to Reno to establish residency for the next six weeks so she can divorce her husband." I recapped.

Stout nodded.

"What about her husband? I can't believe he's in agreement with this?" Harley asked.

"Doesn't really matter what he wants. I haven't spoken to him, but I suspect, once he discovers he stands to get absolutely nothing from the Rollins estate I don't think he will object too strenuously," Stout added with the first trace of a smile since he'd entered the room, but it didn't last long. "I'm here because I wanted to make sure you knew exactly where Samantha Stevens was. She is not in any way attempting to avoid the law." Taking a piece of paper from his pocket, Stout handed over a paper with an address and telephone number. "Here is the location where she will be staying for the next six weeks if you need to get in touch with her."

"This is incredible. We should have her arrested and brought back here." Chief Mike was still boiling mad.

"On what charge? Neither Samantha nor Frank Logan have violated any laws. Samantha Rollins was not under arrest. She cooperated with the investigation fully and intends to continue to cooperate," Stout said wearily. "Just from Reno."

"But what about the funeral?" Harley asked. "If she plans to stay in Reno for six weeks, what about JP Rollins? Harley had managed to hit upon the one person who seemed to have been forgotten in the midst of this mess.

"Gentlemen, I think you'd be hard pressed to find ten people who are sorry that JP Rollins is no longer alive. Once the body is released, we'll have him interred quietly and discreetly."

After a few more questions, Stout pulled himself up from his chair and left.

The rest of us were left to ponder the new situation.

"I suppose it could have been worse." Tim added.

"How on earth could it have been worse?" Harley asked.

"She could have gone to the Dominican Republic. They only have a one day residency requirement." Tim smiled.

CHAPTER 14

Friday night was date night, although with Paris's busy career, we usually went out a bit later than most couples. One of our favorite restaurants was a combination Jazz Club and restaurant called Cesselly's. The food was good, the atmosphere was better. The owners were both retired jazz musicians, well known and well respected in the jazz community. Their names attracted some of the best musicians in the country. It wasn't uncommon to have big name musicians drop by on their way to a show in Chicago or Detroit and sit down and jam with their old friends. Cesselly's had live music every night, whether from a jazz pianist, a small local trio or a Grammy-winning superstar. Both Paris and I loved jazz but apart from that, Cesselly's held special significance as the place where we had our first date.

Tonight, the featured entertainer was a local artist, Jerome Davis, who had just started to make a name for himself as a jazz pianist with a small trio. Paris had known Jerome in high school. I didn't realize how well she'd known him until he took a break and came over to the table.

"I couldn't believe my eyes when I saw you sitting out there." Jerome gave Paris a big hug and a long kiss on the cheek.

"I didn't know you would be performing until we got here, but it's good to see you again." Paris smile was strained as she pulled away from his embrace and turned to face me. "Jerome, let me introduce you. This is RJ Franklin. RJ, this is Jerome Davis."

We shook hands and Jerome pulled up a chair and sat down, a little too close to Paris for my liking.

"I loved the set. You must be doing pretty well for yourself." Paris added, keeping the conversation rolling while Jerome smiled and stared at Paris and gave me an occasional glance.

"Things are going very well. My second CD hit the top ten in Europe."

"That's great. Isn't it RJ?" Paris was trying so hard to include me in the conversation when possible.

"Great." I mumbled.

Jerome didn't notice. He seemed more intent on taking long strolls down memory lane, reminiscing about the days when they were a couple; which he seemed to think exceptionally interesting.

"Did you know this girl used to be the love of my life?" Jerome looked at me.

"You don't say."

It's not easy to make a black person blush, but I saw the color rising to Paris' face. "Jerome always loved to exaggerate. I was hardly the love of your life. We both know your one and only love is music," Paris joked, trying to lighten the mood.

"Well, that is true. I do love music. But that was the wonderful thing about us as a couple. I could play and you could sing. We always made beautiful music together."

Jerome smiled, but then leaned in, "Are you still singing?"

"Only at church." Paris added, relieved to notice that the rest of the trio were starting to make their way back to the stage. "Looks like your break is just about over. I'm glad you came over to say hi."

"Hey! How about one song for ole time sake?" Jerome pleaded.

Paris did a good job of politely pushing him away and before long he was back on stage. But Jerome wasn't done. After dedicating his next song to his old flame, which was sitting in the audience, he then proceeded to coax her to come up on stage to sing. With the support of the audience, Paris reluctantly rose, mouthed an apology to me. She approached the stage to the applause of the audience.

After a brief consultation, they finally agreed on the tune she would sing, Jerome, somewhat reluctantly, but Paris seemed firm and after a moment with the other members of the band, they started what turned out to be, a jazzy version of an Angela

Winbush tune, "Lay Your Troubles Down." Whether Jerome's reluctance was due to the religious nature of the tune or not, the jazzy music and Paris' strong, vocals were a huge hit with the audience.

She had an excellent voice. She was a strong alto with a deep, rich tone that reminded me of Anita Baker or Dianne Reeves. One of her greatest attributes was a very large range which allowed her to hit extremely high notes when necessary. Paris called it an ability to scream on pitch and said she couldn't comfortably maintain the notes for an extended period of time; but she definitely had a gift and she knew how to use it to its fullest advantage. She used her voice like a carpenter used tools and it was a pleasure to listen to her.

The song ended to a standing ovation, and while Jerome clearly wanted Paris to continue, she shut him down quickly. She thanked the audience for their kind applause, but let it be known that the audience, including herself, had come to hear the band, and she retired to her table to enjoy the rest of the performance.

She tried to enjoy the performance but I could tell she just wasn't into it. After about 30 more minutes I leaned across and asked if she was okay.

She nodded. "Yes. Just frustrated. Would you like to leave?"

I knew the question was rhetorical. It was obvious she was ready to leave. So, I paid the bill and we slipped out.

Jerome noticed our departure and motioned for us to wait, but Paris shook her head, blew a kiss to him and grabbed my arm as we marched out the door.

The car ride to her house was silent. When we arrived, we sat for a few minutes in silence while she gathered her thoughts.

After a few moments, she turned to me. "I'm sorry, but I want to apologize about Jerome. He has been like this as long as I've known him."

"Nothing to apologize for—" I was halted by the look in her eyes.

She took a deep breath. "Yes there is. He was rude to you and implied there was more to our relationship than there actually was. We dated, briefly when I was in high school. He was a couple years older than me and I was flattered an 'older man' was interested in me. It didn't take long before I realized his interest wasn't exactly in me, if you know what I mean. Like all teenage boys, he was only interested in sex. His other interests revolved around his band and a huge desire to get out of St. Joe and make a name for himself. We went out a few times, talked on the phone, and then when I surprised him by showing up at one of his gigs and found him with one of his many other girlfriends, that was it."

"You don't owe me an explanation."

"I wanted you to know."

I pulled her close and took her in my arms. I kissed her until I felt the tension in her body relax. When we pulled apart, she snuggled up like kitten. When we finally got out of the car, she was almost back to normal.

At the door, she reached up and kissed me.

I held her tight for several minutes then whispered in her ear, "Thank you. You just saved me a ton of trouble."

She pulled back and stared with a puzzled expression.

"Now I won't have to go back to the precinct and issue a warrant for his arrest."

Saturday morning was a beautiful day. The MAC-U Raiders were playing away this week, and they were expected to win handily. The day turned out to be one of those truly remarkable autumn days where the weather was cool, but not cold—sweater weather. Autumn in St. Joe was my favorite time of year. It was football season and I loved football. I loved the fall foliage with golden, rust and burgundy colored leaves that blanketed yards and roads. The trees put on a vibrant display of colors, from pale golden yellow to rich merlot and practically everything in between. I especially liked to go downtown St. Joe and spend time on the East Race where the St. Joseph River curved around the city and admire the beautiful landscape.

Before my car accident, I used to run. I ran the path along the East Race and watched white water rafters traverse the rapids while I ran along the pathway. After the accident, I had to face the reality that running was no longer in the cards for me. Not only was it bad for my knee, but after several surgeries and a metal plate, I realized it just wasn't worth the pain and damage. So, instead of running, I bought a bicycle. At first, I didn't think I'd enjoy it, but I found biking provided great exercise that was low-impact, but it still allowed me to spend time outside. The East Race was a four mile journey, round trip and provided a great opportunity to enjoy the sights and sounds of the city.

The only thing that would have made this day better would have been spending it with Paris. However, Saturdays were a busy time for hair stylist, especially for Black Women. For Christians, Saturday represented the last opportunity to get your hair styled before Sunday's church service. For the party animals, Saturday represented the last opportunity to get your hair styled before a night of partying at the clubs. Whether saint or sinner Saturdays meant big money for hair stylist.

However, I had enough things to occupy my mind. Personally, things were going well. My relationship with Paris was flourishing. We'd been dating for several months, but her birthday was approaching and I was undecided about what to give her. I knew her well enough to know she wouldn't accept an expensive present. She wasn't the type to be impressed by money. She preferred handmade gifts over store-bought gifts any day of the week, but crafts weren't my thing. She was renovating her house and I loved working with wood. I thought of making something for her home, but would a new mantel or a bookshelf really say, '*I think you're special?*' Shopping was one of my least favorite things and the thought of having to go to the mall made my head hurt. So, I was thankful when my phone rang.

I was surprised to see Judge Browning's number appear. I was even more surprised when he asked if I was available to come by his home later this afternoon. We agreed on a time and after I hung up, I had something new to occupy my thoughts. I wondered if the visit was related to my class. Had I deluded myself that things were going better than they really were? Had the parents been in touch with him to demand their sons and daughters get taught by 'real' tenured academic professors of law rather than a two-bit cop? The more I thought about it, the more I convinced myself my teaching days were over. It came as a bit of a surprise when I realized I would miss it. Once I got over the initial fear, I'd found the students stimulating and the questions and energy they exuded were a bit of a rush. But, I would have more time for work and other things without spending my nights reviewing lesson plans and preparing for lectures. It had only been a week, but I'd enjoyed it. Nevertheless, I'd warned him before he hired me.

Later that afternoon, I found myself sitting in the same chair in E.L. Browning's comfortable study, as I had just a few days earlier. I declined the offer of tea this time and just waited for the axe to fall. Judge Browning looked uncomfortable and kept picking invisible pieces of lint from his sleeve while we sat and made small talk for a few moments before he finally said, "I know you're probably wondering why I asked you to come by."

"Not really. I've been expecting it."

Judge Browning's head snapped up and the look in his eyes told me I'd misjudged his intention.

"What do you mean?"

Shifting position, both literally and figuratively, I said, "You're firing me, right?"

I think E.L. laughed for at least two full minutes before he finally squeaked out, "No such luck my boy. Sorry, but I've heard nothing but raves from your students. In fact, I have at least six requests from students who took the class last semester who want to audit the class and others who are ineligible, but want me to bend the rules and extend the add date so they can add your class even though the deadline is passed."

"You're making that up." I tried to hide the smile in my voice.

He shook his head. "Sorry. You are a huge success. Just like I knew you would be. You've got a great perspective these young people need to hear. For too many young lawyers, the law is something they read about in books. It's not real. It's theories and cases and briefs and legal jargon. Thanks to you, they're seeing the law as it really is." He leaned forward. "It's people, not rules. Our laws were intended to serve the people, but we've turned it into something cold and impersonal." E.L. got up from his chair and paced the floor as he'd done so many times as a practicing defense attorney many decades earlier.

"The law was written to protect the people. But, we've turned the law into something above the people—we've made it into something people can't touch or feel and have taken the feelings out of the law. In my opinion that's why so few people respect the law. Instead of the law serving man, we've made men servants to the law."

"I can tell you've thought about this." I said.

He laughed. "Maybe once or twice." He returned to his chair. "I'm sorry, I don't mean to lecture."

"That's ok. I hope one day, I can speak half as eloquently and passionately as you do."

"You already do. Remember, I watched you."

I was flattered, but slightly confused. "If you didn't ask me here to fire me, why did you ask me, if I may be so bold?"

Judge Browning had always been a strong force on the bench. My fellow officers and I may not have agreed with all of his decisions, but he had a reputation for being fair. So, he'd earned our respect. I was a bit puzzled by the hesitation I saw him displaying now. After a deep breath, he started.

"When you came to me for information about JP Rollins murder, I told you the truth…technically. However, I withheld a bit of information."

"*What?*"

The look on his face, more than the hand he held up, stopped me from saying more.

"I know what you are going to say, but after you hear what I'm about to tell you, I hope you will understand my reasoning."

He sat silently for a moment, and then took a deep breath. "JP Rollins was a mean, hateful, vindictive man. He was tough as nails and proud of it. I knew his wife, Marie. She and my wife, Carol, were friends. Marie had been active in the Civil Rights Movement." E.L. paused for a moment and looked out the window, as if looking back in time. After a few moments, he continued. "Marie marched and fought beside Carol and me through many battles. She was arrested and threatened. Who knows, maybe she suffered more than we did. The names she was called were just as bad as some of the ones we were called. At least for us, we had the support of the African American community. Half of the African Americans resented her participation and the others didn't trust her. She met JP and fell head over heels in love. For a while, I think it was good. Maybe he loved her too, if he was capable of love." E.L. stopped for a few moments.

I could tell this was extremely hard for him, so I waited patiently until he was ready to continue.

He sighed. "I think the changes started after she miscarried for the third or fourth time. JP started to work more and more hours. She wanted a baby so badly. Carol and I had our two boys and a baby on the way. You know, Marie was my daughter, Maya's godmother…and well, I think not being able to have their own children was putting a strain on the marriage. I think she tried to talk to JP but he didn't want to go to the doctor. He blamed her." He shrugged. "Whatever the reason, they grew apart. JP started working longer and longer hours, growing his business. Marie needed someone to talk to. So…she turned to Charles."

Interrupting, I wanted to make sure I was clear on the facts. "Charles was JP's brother?"

E.L. nodded. "Yes. Charles was younger and a lot nicer. He was everything JP wasn't, patient, understanding…kind. Before either one of them knew what was happening, they were in love and miserable. I know Marie asked for a divorce but JP refused."

"Are you trying to say its JP Rollin's fault his wife and his brother had an affair?" I didn't care for JP Rollins but my family instilled in me each man was responsible for his own actions. I wasn't feeling sympathetic toward Marie or Charles at this point.

E.L. shook his head before adding, "No. I'm not blaming JP or Marie or Charles. I'm merely telling a story." He took a deep breath. "Once the affair started, they knew they couldn't continue. Marie found out she was pregnant and that's when she and Charles decided to run away together. I believe Carol and I were the only people Marie told they were going. And she swore us to secrecy. In fact, I haven't told another living soul about this…until now."

He sat silently for a moment and then shook his head and continued. "They ran off together. JP was furious. I'm sure he must have felt humiliated and angry. He tried everything. He used to come over here ranting he knew we knew where they were. But we didn't say a word. You'd think he would have given up and gotten over it, but not JP Rollins. About six months after they were gone, Carol went into labor and had Maya. Marie had already had Samantha. She was so proud. She wanted us to see the baby. So, she and Charles snuck back into town."

"You saw her?" I asked.

He nodded.

"It was November 2nd, Maya's birthday. They were leaving when a young, attorney who had had a few too many drinks crashed into them."

E.L. looked as though he were looking back in time, reliving the events from twenty years ago.

"The police report said it was a hit and run. The driver was never found." I said softly.

E.L. paused several moments before adding. "The driver WAS found. His name was…is…Richard Stout."

CHAPTER 15

"*RICHARD STOUT!* JP Rollins attorney?"

E.L. nodded. "We worked together many times in the past, so when he was in need of help, he came to me. But, I had a conflict of interest. I couldn't represent him."

"I don't understand. How is it none of this information is in the police report?"

"Because when JP Rollins found out about it, he used all his money and power to work a deal. No charges were ever filed against Stout. In exchange, Stout worked for JP Rollins.

The words Richard Stout said when asked why he worked for a man like JP Rollins came back to me, '*when you sell your soul to the devil.*'

"Let me get this straight. While driving intoxicated, Richard Stout killed JP Rollins wife and brother and then worked for him for over twenty years and no one thought this worth mentioning, when JP was found with a knife in his chest?"

"I'm telling you now." He held up his hands. "The case was dropped. No charges were ever brought against Stout. I don't know if too many people are around today that know all of the details of what really happened that many years ago."

I was pacing by now, trying to process all of this information. "So you think JP Rollins was holding this over Stout's head for all these years?"

"RJ, I truly don't know. But I can't think of any other reason why Stout continued to work for a Son of a—" He shook himself. "A man like JP Rollins."

"I need to talk to Mr. Stout."

We tried to reach Richard Stout all weekend. After unsuccessfully trying to reach Stout by phone, I decided to try my luck by showing up on his doorstep.

Richard Stout lived in one of the apartment complexes on the north end of town. Tulip Trail Apartments was a large, development built in the 1970s. Instead of the massive, high rise apartment buildings that were common in that period, Tulip Trail had smaller, four-unit buildings, two upper and two lower units in each building. None of the buildings were exactly alike although they all had the same basic layout. Whether by paint, architectural embellishments, or facades of brick, stone or vinyl, the buildings each had some unique detail which differentiated each one from its neighbor. Inside the units all had two bedrooms, a decent sized living area, large eat-in kitchens, in unit washer and dryers, and either an outside patio or balcony. There were also two single car garages on each side, although the wait list could be quite long for one of these. The development also had plenty of exterior parking. The nicest point, in my mind, was the units didn't share walls; they were separated by a hallway which minimized noise. I knew a lot about Tulip Trails because I lived there after I graduated from college. As a young policeman, they were quite appealing. I'd lived there until I purchased my townhouse about five years ago.

Richard Stout's building was near the back of the complex and butted up to a nearby park. There was the standard intercom security system, but I knew a trick which gained me access to the interior hallway; which I utilized when Stout failed to answer the intercom.

Inside, I knocked several times but Stout never answered. I lucked out, when the neighbor across the hall came out.

Mr. Howard Banner was an elderly gentleman of 86 years old. Howard was initially reluctant to share information but after I flashed my shield, he invited me inside to share a cup of coffee and some of the cookies his great granddaughter baked for his birthday.

Mr. Banner's unit, which was more than likely a mirror image of Richard Stout's, was cramped with old, overstuffed furniture. Nearly every surface was plastered with pictures that told the story of his 86 years along with that of his now deceased wife, five brothers, two sisters, six children, fourteen grand children and 57 great-grand children. Mr. Banner had served in World War II and been awarded a purple heart for a bullet which was lodged too closely to his spine to be removed and he still carried to this day. Banner joked the bullet never caused him any pain but if he sat too closely to the television it ruined his reception.

After forty-five minutes of engaging conversation with a nice, but somewhat lonely man, I left Tulip Trails with the knowledge Richard Stout had left Friday evening with a small duffle. He'd asked Banner to get his mail and newspaper until he could get the services halted, and had given him an address where he could be reached in the event of an emergency. Banner felt the police showing up at the door constituted an emergency, so he passed along the address.

Looking at the address, I knew in my gut that the murder of JP Rollins had just gotten even more complicated.

CHAPTER 16

Sunday morning found me sitting in early service next to Mama B, who was looking quite nautical in navy blue and white with a large, white three-pointed sailor's cap with a large rhinestone broach on the front. Today was the fourth Sunday and Paris was singing with the Gospel Chorus. She led an updated version of the traditional spiritual, *Sometimes I Feel Like a Motherless Child*, which had the entire church on their feet. The familiar words seemed especially poignant as I thought of Samantha Stevens.

Sometimes I Feel Like a Motherless Child
Sometimes I feel like a motherless child
Sometimes I feel like a motherless child
Sometimes I feel like a motherless child
A long ways from home
A long ways from home
True believer
A long ways from home
Along ways from home

Samantha Stevens was a motherless child, just like the slaves who penned the original song. She may not have suffered the same horrors of being bought and sold like cattle, having your offspring ripped from your arms along with your dignity and all of the other atrocities that went along with slavery, but I suspected the feeling of loneliness were the same. For a moment, I thought about how much I missed my own mother. I was fortunate. I was an adult when my mom died. I'd been blessed to have been raised by two loving, caring parents. Plus, I had a sibling, my sister. In addition to my blood family, I had a tight-knit church family. I stole a glance at Mama B just in time

to see a tear roll down her face. I pulled out my handkerchief
and pushed it into her hand, and then put my arm around her
shoulder and pulled her close. Yes, I was very blessed.

It took a good ten minutes before the congregation was
ready to move on to receive the sermon and even then, there
were still a number of people crying, rocking and occasionally
shouting praises of '*Thank you Jesus*' or '*Bless His Name*.' Paris
had a wonderful gift which was a lot more than her vocal ability.
She had what our Pastor, Rev. Hilton V. Hamilton called, '*The
Anointing*.' I'm not sure I know the right words to describe
what that means or what really happened when she sang,
especially when she sang in church. You'd have to experience
it to fully understand. In basic terms, I'd say she sang like she
really meant it. She was able to touch your emotions. It was as
though certain notes touched something inside you and started
a vibration. Whatever it was, she definite had it.

The young man who directed the choir was the first of the
candidates for the Minister of Music position at the church. Within
the limited time frame of the early service, he demonstrated his
ability to select music to compliment the message; he directed the
choir and showcased his ability to play the organ. I'd say he was
off to a rousing start. He wasn't as young as the previous Choir
Director and that was a mark in his favor in the minds of many,
including Mama B. He was married and he introduced his wife to
the congregation, which was another mark in his favor. Although
the last Choir Director had also been married, the congregation
hadn't realize that until his wife showed up at the church, eighteen
months after his arrival and a couple of weeks before he was
murdered. Filling high profile staff positions in the twenty-first
century church was a pretty complicated endeavor. Although,
perhaps if Jesus had interrogated the disciples, or had someone
investigating their backgrounds, he would have known about
Peter's proclivity to swear, Thomas's doubtful nature, and Judas's
treasonous nature. I smiled at the very idea, even though I knew
foreknowledge wouldn't have changed His selection two thousand
years ago, or today. He knew all of our dirt, shortcomings and
weaknesses and loved us anyway.

Reverend Hamilton's message was one of love and acceptance. He preached of a forgiving, understanding God who accepted each of us, just as we were. After service, Paris and I enjoyed a wonderful dinner of smothered chicken, mashed potatoes, and lima beans with Mama B.

We sat on the front porch and watched the basketball game at the rec center while Mama B told stories from the Mother's Board Meeting. If Paris's gift was music, Mama B's gift was in storytelling. She was able to make the most mundane of events interesting and funny. Paris and I laughed at the debate the Mother's Board had about ways to raise money for the Pastor's Anniversary. Apparently, there was concern Greater Mount Zion's Mother's Board had raised over two thousand dollars for their Pastor's Anniversary and were boasting about it at the regional meeting. Greater Mount Zion had a population half the size of FBC and most of the members felt it would reflect poorly on Reverend Hamilton if they couldn't raise twice as much.

"Two Thousand dollars is a lot of money," Paris said.

Mama B rocked. "Pshaw."

"You don't believe they raised that much?" I asked.

Mama B rocked.

Paris glanced in my direction.

"Now, come on. You can't tell me you think they lied about how much they raised?" I teased.

Mama B rocked and refused to make eye contact. She had a smile on her face that said what she refused to say out loud.

"You're telling me the good Christian women of Greater Mount Zion lied about how much money they raised?" I prodded.

Mama B rocked for several moments. "I ain't saying they lied." She rocked. "But that Mother's Board ain't bit more raised two thousand dollars than a man in the moon."

I smiled at Mama B's idiom. She was from Mississippi and had a lot of sayings that made me stop and think. *Bit More* and *A Man in the Moon* were two of them.

"Well, look-at that." She rocked.

Paris and I followed Mama B's gaze and saw a car drive down the street in front of the rec center. The car blew its horn and we automatically waved. We watched as the car turned and came down the alley and pulled up behind my car.

I stared as a short, thin older man in his early sixties got out of the car. He was dark-skinned, with a small white afro and side burns that were popular in the 1970s and a thick, white moustache that reminded me of a walrus. Reverend Cleophus Jefferson was the pastor of Greater Mount Zion Missionary Baptist Church. He not only looked like a pimp from the 1970, but walked, talked and acted like it. He had on polyester pants, white shoes, a large white belt and a loud, floral polyester shirt that was open at the neck showcasing several large gold necklaces.

"Good evening, Saints." Reverend Cleophus Jefferson smiled broadly and walked up to the porch rail.

"Evening Reverend, Take this chair and I'll go get another one." I stood and prepared to go into the house to bring out another chair, but was halted.

"No, Brother RJ, I can't stay. I just wanted to stop by and holla at Sister Ella." He smiled at Mama B."

She smiled and rocked. "We was just talking about you, and here you are."

He laughed. "I hope it was all good things."

Mama B avoided responding by pointing to Paris. "Reverend, have you met, Sister Williams?"

Paris smiled and held out a hand.

Reverend Jefferson smiled like a crocodile, took her hand in his and then brought it to his lips and kissed it."

I could tell by the rise in her eyebrows and the questioning look in her eyes, she had been shocked by the move.

"Now, Reverend, I would hate to have to arrest a man of the cloth," I joked.

Reverend Jefferson jumped back and made an elaborate gesture of demonstrating he was keeping his hands off by holding up both hands.

We laughed. I knew Reverend Jefferson had a huge crush on Mama B, who couldn't have cared less for him. His unrequited advances were probably what kept him coming back. I suspected he viewed her as a challenge.

After a few minutes of small talk, I wondered how Mama B would steer the conversation to the anniversary.

"I heard you had a really successful anniversary," she said when there was a lull in the conversation.

"Yes, Ma'am. God is good all the time." He nodded.

"I heard you might need some protection?" I volunteered.

He stared with a question in his eyes.

"Mama B was telling me your church raised so much money, you better be careful driving around town without a police escort." I joked.

Reverend Jefferson laughed. "Well, I appreciate the offer Brother RJ. Yes, I am truly blessed. I have a small congregation, but they were extremely generous, extremely generous." He nodded and smiled.

I was just about to give up hope he'd volunteer the actual amount raised, when he surprised me. "Yes, God has been so good. I don't have as large of a congregation as First Baptist Church and my members aren't college educated, but they dug deep and made sacrifices and gave me over two thousand dollar. That's more money than we take in for an entire month of services. Yes, the Lord is good and I'm so thankful."

Mama B smiled like a cat that's just devoured a bowl of cream.

Reverend Jefferson stayed a few minutes longer and then got in his car and drove away.

Mama B rocked. "I knew they was lying."

"Maybe they were confused," Paris said.

"They was confused alright." She rocked and smiled.

Paris and I stayed and talked a little longer until the mosquitoes got too bad and then we headed home with our Tupperware to enjoy the remainder of our Sunday afternoon. However this Sunday's walk in the park would be somewhat different.

CHAPTER 17

After Judge Browning's bombshell Saturday night, I went home and made two phone calls. The first was to Harley and the second was to Chief Mike. I can't say how many calls Chief Mike made, but I knew at least one of them was to the District Attorney. The outcome of all of the calls was Harley and I were going to make an attempt to interview Richard Stout. Whether we'd be able to do it or not was questionable because the address he'd given to his neighbor was for St. Joseph Rehab Center.

St. Joe Rehab was a large facility located near downtown. It was a sprawling complex with multiple buildings and was actually a huge regional facility which handled everything from substance abuse to dementia. There were buildings for housing mentally disturbed youth as well as adults and they provided a plethora of services to the community. Richard Stout had checked himself into the building for chemical dependency. We were being allowed in to see him but whether or not he would answer questions, was going to be up to him and his physician.

Several members of the congregation were residents in the nursing home section, so I left Paris visiting with some of them while I met Harley a few floors up in the wing for Chemical Dependencies.

Like me, Harley was dressed in his Sunday best. Neither one of us had gone home to change after church. Visiting hours were limited and neither one of us wanted to waste the time it would take to change clothes, so we were both rather more formal than usual. One of the interesting things I noticed about the differences between African American Churches and Caucasian churches in Indiana was the dress code was more relaxed in the Caucasian churches than that worn at African-American churches. There used to be a time when going to church on Sundays was more like a fashion show than a place of worship. Growing up, my sister and I had school clothes and church clothes. Our church clothes were more formal. I didn't believe God cared two figs what people wore to worship. However, going to church was a special occasion and the congregation dressed accordingly. Older women like Mama B wore hats and their best outfits to church. It was a sign of respect and reverence, however things were changing. Now, it wasn't uncommon to see people wearing blue jeans or even shorts to Sunday church service. However, older congregations, like FBC still leaned towards more formal attire. Having been raised in the South, Harley shared many of the same traditions as the African American churches. Although his church was a lot less formal, he said he just didn't feel right if he wasn't wearing a suit on Sunday. I guess that's another reason Mama B liked him.

The Chemical Dependency Wing attempted through paint and décor to look less like a sterile hospital and more of a cool lounge. There were comfortable chairs and large televisions in the communal areas. Walking down the halls, we looked into the rooms, which very much resembled the standard hospital environments with bed, chair, desk and lamp. We stopped at the nurses' station and asked a large big buxom woman with pencil drawn eyebrows for Stout's room. She smiled and took our shields and compared the names with a list on the computer. We must have been cleared because she nodded and pointed us to the end of the hall.

Stout's door was open, but we knocked anyway before entering.

"Come in Officers." Stout said as we walked softly into the room.

Stout had a small, private room with a single bed, a couple of guest chairs and a desk. There was one small window that looked out on the parking lot, but nothing else of interest or personality in the room.

Once in the room, we were greeted by Stout's doctor, Dr. Hall. Hall was tall, thin and looked like he'd be more comfortable riding a surfboard than navigating around a hospital. Maybe it was the loud Hawaiian shirt, plaid shorts, Birkenstocks or the pony tail that hung to his waist. Whatever the reason, Dr. Hall seemed like the type that might be in need of the Chemical Dependency Wing rather than running it. Stout performed the introductions.

"Dr. Hall, Detectives Franklin and Wickfield, two of St. Joe's finest."

The comments were said with little feeling but that might have been due to the fact that Stout looked like all of his energies were required for controlling his shaking hands, none could be wasted on niceties.

We shook hands.

Dr. Hall wasted no time in setting the boundaries for our visit with crisp, military precision he laid down the law. "Gentleman I told your Chief *and* the District Attorney I am not at all in favor of this interrogation of my patient. Mr. Stout is very ill and is in a delicate condition. I want it clearly understood you are to have a total of fifteen minutes and he is not to be upset."

We nodded our acknowledgement of the rules.

Dr. Hall turned to speak to Stout before leaving. "Please push the control if you need me or if things become too much." He turned to look at us. "Although, I hope that won't be necessary."

Stout nodded.

Dr. Hall turned to face Harley and me and held up his watch. We nodded and he walked out.

I was shocked at the decline I'd seen in Richard Stout in just the past two days. He looked bad in the District Attorney's office, but he looked like he'd aged about twenty years in the past two days.

My shock must have registered on my face because Stout laughed, or tried to laugh. It came out more as a grimace. "They don't allow mirrors in these places so you can't see how bad you look. But if your faces are any indication, I must look pretty bad." Each word seemed an effort and he shivered like a man who was freezing. His teeth chattered and his hands shook uncontrollably.

I hadn't noticed the lack of mirrors until Stout mentioned it, but briefly glanced around and realized he was right. But we didn't have much time and I didn't want to waste it in small talk. Harley and I took seats in the guest chairs. Harley took out his notebook.

"Mr. Stout, we are sorry to bother you. But we need to know what happened with you and JP Rollins," I said

Stout nodded. He held up a hand to prevent me from continuing and said, "It might be easier if you just let me talk for now. I haven't had any medicine to ease the shakes so my mind will be clear, but I'm going to need something soon."

I nodded.

"On November 2nd twenty years ago, I had just won a big case. I went out to celebrate. I had been drinking and smoking and…well… you get the picture. I got in my car to drive home. It had just started to snow and the roads were slippery and wet. It was dark and I was driving…too fast for the road conditions. I was coming around a curve and saw the headlights too late." He reached for a cup of water on the nightstand by his desk. The shaking was so bad, I was sure he would spill it and almost got up to help him, but thought better of it. Even a man in his condition had his dignity.

Eventually, he got the cup and took a couple of sips then replaced the cup on the nightstand. The effort seemed to wear him out. He leaned back in his chair and took a couple of deep breaths. "I was young and scared. I knew I'd lose my license, probably go to jail. It was overwhelming. And then I met JP Rollins. He was a mean S.O.B. He actually thanked me for '*cleaning up his dirty laundry*.' He said he could arrange things so my career would be saved…arrange things so I wouldn't go to jail. He promised me a job working for him."

"Why?" Harley asked. "Why do all of that for a stranger."

Stout shook his head and shrugged. "At the time, I thought he didn't want the embarrassment of people finding out his wife left him. After twenty years of doing his dirty work, I think he just wanted a slave. JP liked control. He held that over my head. He wouldn't let me leave. I was forced to work for him exclusively."

"Mr. Stout. Did you kill JP Rollins?"

He paused so long I wondered if he intended to answer, but eventually, he just shook his head. "I wanted to so many times. But, I didn't have the guts. I saw what it looked like and what it felt like to kill those two poor people all those years ago. I couldn't intentionally do that to anyone… not even JP Rollins." His hand shook more and he clasped them together to stop the shaking. "I have had to live with the nightmares for twenty years."

Nightmares I understood.

At that moment the door opened and Dr. Hall came into the room just far enough to hold the door open for us. Taking the not very subtle clue, Harley and I rose to leave. We halted as Stout continued.

"I haven't had a drink or taken more than an aspirin since that night. But, after JP Rollins was murdered, I felt such a relief. I had to celebrate. I just…"

"Thank you Mr. Stout for talking to us." I extended a hand to him. Stout hesitated briefly before extending his hand and we shook.

"Detective," Stout called just before I walked out.

I walked back into the room.

"One thing. You might want to talk to Michelle Hopewell again."

"The bridesmaid?" I must have looked as puzzled as I felt.

He nodded. "Yeah. She called a few days ago wanting to know if she can prove she was carrying JP Rollin's baby if she would be entitled to a portion of his estate."

Outside, Harley and I found Paris sitting on a bench watching children playing in an enclosed playground.

"What do you think happened to him? I mean he seemed just fine a few days ago." Harley said.

"When I talked to his neighbor, he said Mr. Stout had been fine for years, no signs of anything wrong until a couple of weeks ago. That's when he noticed whiskey bottles and beer cans in the trash outside his door. He stopped going to work as he had in the past and would come home late and stayed in, drinking and probably doing drugs."

"What do you think about Michelle Hopewell? Do you really believe she's pregnant by her friend's father? This is starting to sound like a Jerry Springer episode." Harley said.

"I don't know but I think we're going to find out."

CHAPTER 18

Harley and I spent the first part of Monday morning in meetings and catching up on the paperwork that had accumulated over the weekend. By noon, we were seated in the living room at the Hopewell home. Michelle Hopewell was excited and talking ninety miles per hour. According to her, her mourning had now been turned to joy. She practically radiated and the tears and sniffles from our last interview were now replaced with a nervous giggle.

"Miss Hopewell, we understand congratulations are in order." Harley again took the lead in the interview while I took a seat on the plastic covered sofa.

"Isn't it wonderful?" She patted her stomach and giggled.

"Hmm… When is the joyous day?"

"Oh, the doctor said it will most likely be early March. They think I'm two months pregnant. That's about the last time JP and I…well." Michelle giggled. "You know. So that's probably when it happened. Normally, we were pretty careful."

"How long had you and JP Rollins been…ah…dating." Harley tried delicacy although I doubt if she appreciated his efforts or even recognized it.

"Well, I don't know if you can really call it dating. We didn't exactly go out to dinner and movies or anything like that. But one day about a year ago, I was at the house waiting for Sam and JP was there and we started talking. He'd been drinking a bit and seemed a bit tipsy. And, well, he just came right out and grabbed me." Michelle seemed positively giddy.

"And that was the start of your…relationship?" Harley tried to get her on track.

She nodded. "After that, he would call me about once or twice a week and we would meet somewhere and well…you know." She giggled.

Yeah. I knew exactly what JP Rollins was doing. I didn't think Michelle would like the name I had for it.

"And no one knew about the two of you?"

She shook her head. "No. JP said it might not look good for his image because I was so young and all. But, I was over eighteen and so it was legal and everything. Right?"

Harley tugged at his collar. "You were of age for consensual sex."

"That's what I told him. But he said no. Anyway, I kept my mouth shut just liked he wanted."

"What did Samantha think about you and JP being together?" Harley asked.

She stared wide eyed. "She didn't know. But, I'm sure she wouldn't have cared. I mean…why should she?"

Why indeed. I tried to make sure my mask hid the thoughts that floated through my head.

"You said two months ago was the last time that you two were…intimate. Why was that?"

Michelle hesitated here, and for the first time, the giggling stopped. "JP stopped calling."

"Did you call him?"

Michelle shook her head. "He told me I wasn't to call him… EVER! So, I didn't. I just waited."

"You never asked him why he stopped calling?" Harley asked.

Michelle shook her head. "I thought maybe he was busy. There were all of his businesses and the wedding and…I just thought I'd wait."

"You're a very patient woman." Harley added.

Michelle giggled.

I struggled to keep from gagging while I tried to contemplate how anyone could be that naïve. I leaned forward to try and keep my back from sticking to the plastic. "What did Mr. Rollins have to say about the prospect of becoming a father?"

Michelle looked surprised. I wondered if she'd forgotten I was there. She paused several moments before answering. "I didn't get a chance to tell him. I was hoping we might be able to talk at the reception, but…well, he died. So, he never knew about the baby." Michelle hesitated before looking up. Her eyes filled with tears. "I think that's sad. He never knew he was going to be a father, for real this time. Not just adopting like he did with Samantha but a real father." She sniffed and looked at me as though she expected some type of answer.

I didn't have a response to that one.

Harley asked, "I hate to sound…indelicate, but are you positive Mr. Rollins is the father?"

Michelle giggled. "That's the same question that lawyer guy asked. And I'll tell you the same thing I told him. There's only one way to get a baby and JP Rollins was the only person that I've done *that* with, so it has to be his baby!"

I couldn't argue with her logic.

"How do you think Samantha will take the news?" Harley asked.

Michelle beamed, "I think she'll be glad. She always hated being an only child. Now she won't be anymore. I can't wait until she comes back, so I can tell her the good news."

Harley asked a few additional questions and between the giggles, we didn't get a lot of concrete information to help us with our murder investigation.

Back at the station, we were told Kelly Lyston was waiting for us in one of the conference rooms. We entered the conference room and stopped at the sight that greeted us. The cobalt blue haired maid of honor had bruises covering her face and upper arms that matched the color of her hair. Her lip was cut and swollen and she looked like she'd just spent a couple rounds in the ring with Muhammad Ali.

Most people would have asked what happened. They might have suggested she'd been in a car accident or fallen down a flight of stairs. But, I've been in this business too long. I've seen too many women come through those doors with similar bruises and scars and I recognized that look in her eyes the moment she looked at me.

Harley looked dazed while I could feel myself seething with anger. I had absolutely no tolerance for a man that would hit a woman. My parents were old fashioned. When I turned sixteen and was allowed to go out on dates, my dad took me aside and had '*the talk with me.*' That talk covered everything from sex to marriage and parenthood. It lasted about five minutes all told. My dad was a man of few words. He told me if I got a girl pregnant I'd better be prepared to marry her. If I made a baby, then I'd better be prepared to support it because he had raised his children and didn't intend to raise mine. I needed to treat every woman I dated the same way I would want someone to treat my sister. And if I ever raised my hand to hit a woman, as God was his witness, he'd make sure it was the last thing I'd ever do on this side of Glory. That pretty much covered my talk about the birds and the bees, what it meant to be a man and how to treat women. Short, sweet and to the point. That was my dad. I took his advice to heart and even though my dad was no longer on this earth, I still honored what he taught me.

I felt sick to my stomach looking at Kelly Lyston and I knew before she opened her mouth she was going to defend him.

"I look like crap. You don't have to say it." Her swollen lip caused her to lisp and she was having a lot of trouble looking me in the eyes.

It took me several seconds to bury the angry words that came to my mind. Finally, I said, "Where is he?"

"Jail. The cops arrested him. Neighbors called the police."

"Good." I paced.

"He didn't mean to—"

I held up my hand for silence. I wasn't in the mood. "Don't you dare sit there and defend him to me." The words came out sharp like bullets from a gun.

"It looks worse than it is." She tried to joke.

"Why are you here Mrs. Lyston?" I sat down and stared at her.

She looked around the room like a caged rat. She looked everywhere but in my eyes. Eventually, she hung her head and mumbled, "I was hoping you could help." She paused and then hurried on, "It was my fault. I deserved it. I pushed his buttons. He's really jealous and sometimes I push him and he…"

I stood up. "Mrs. Lyston, there is absolutely nothing you can say that will convince me to help you get your husband out of jail. He is exactly where he belongs. My job as a policeman is to serve and protect. The best way I can accomplish that for you is to make sure your husband stays where he is."

I walked to the door, wrenched it open and marched down the hall. I was so angry I had no idea what I was doing or where I was going. My anger carried me down the stairs and out the door and into my car. When I stopped driving, I was outside of Paris' salon. I don't really remember walking up the stairs. I don't think I stopped at the reception desk. I just went straight back to her office where, thankfully she was sitting alone. Without knocking, I walked into her office. Whether it was the look in my eyes or the expression on my face, I don't know. But, Paris didn't say a word as I approached her I reached for her.

She stood up and walked into my arms.

I held her as tightly as I could. I don't know how long we stood there but eventually, the anger subsided. When I finally released her, she simply looked at me and said, "Do you want to talk?"

Fifteen minutes later we were seated at a table outside the St. Joseph Chocolate Factory having a cup of tea and a scone as I told her about Kelly Lyston. All I could think about was my dad telling me to treat women the way I would want someone to treat my sister. I think if someone had done to my sister or Paris what Tyler Lyston had done to his wife, I probably would have committed a homicide. Paris listened quietly while I talked.

"Has anyone ever hit you?" I don't know why, but I needed to know.

I was surprised to hear her laugh. "Absolutely not. But, I come from a family with some exceptionally strong willed and very proud Black women." She chuckled. "I pity the fool who would try it. My sisters and I have actually talked about domestic violence and how inconceivable it is to us. I think my brother-in-law, London's husband, would be in greater jeopardy of getting beat than she ever would. My sister can be a bit… overbearing." She laughed. "And I've been blessed that none of the men I've been attracted to have ever laid a hand on me. I think they know better. Besides…" she stopped.

"What? You can't just stop there."

"I don't know if I can say this, especially to a cop."

"Completely off the record—unless you are about to confess to a felony, anything you tell me, stays here." I said.

"Well, I have actually thought a great deal about this. What would I do if a man ever did hit me? I mean, you know, you're in the heat of an argument and tempers rise and suddenly, he hits me. Well, I'd probably try to beat the living daylights out of him. But if a man *BEAT* me; I mean seriously BEAT Me…I might actually commit that felony you alluded to a moment ago. I think I'd probably try to take him out."

"I never could understand how women stayed in those situations."

She shrugged. "I think its poor self esteem. If you believe you deserve it then you accept it. Some women are afraid of being alone and are willing to put up with that just so they can have a man in their lives. Personally, I'd rather be alone." She shook her head. "Seriously, I don't know. I'm sure there are lots of reasons why they stay. Fear?" She shrugged. "I have no idea."

Thirty minutes later, I walked her back to her shop. "I'm sorry for interrupting your day like this." I said in the lobby of her salon.

She reached up and kissed me. "It's okay. Thankfully, my client canceled and I had a couple of hours free."

I kissed her good-bye and waved to her receptionist, Amy.

I drove back to the station.

"You alright?" Harley asked.

"Yeah. I just needed to get away."

Harley nodded.

We worked on in silence until I had to leave to go to campus for my class.

Class on Monday was even more packed than the previous Wednesday and the energy and enthusiasm of the students helped to alleviate the funk I'd found myself in. Tonight's lesson was all about interrogation. We talked about different techniques the police used when interrogating alleged criminals and witnesses. Many students still had the idea that modern day police utilized the same techniques they'd seen on television from twenty years ago. Most were surprised to learn that it was common practice to record all interrogations. Several students got in a rather heated debate about interrogation of minors. And before I knew it, we were out of time. I spent another fifteen minutes continuing the debate after class before I finally made my way to my car.

By the time I got home, I was tired but not melancholy and that was a big improvement. I found teaching to be quite pleasant and a totally different experience than I had built up in my head. Of course, it was still early in the semester and I hadn't had to administer a test yet or grade it. Judge Browning had promised me a student assistant to help with grading. But, I wasn't sure I trusted a student to do my grading. Paris said it was my suspicious nature. Maybe she was right. Not trusting was a hazard of the job. It came with the territory. Most people don't see the ugly side of life, but that seemed to be the only side most cops ran into, especially cops who worked homicide.

I was too tired to think much about grades or papers or JP Rollins, or even Kelly and Tyler Lyston. Tomorrow was a new day and I would try to sort through this crazy madness and make sense of it. Tonight, I fell asleep quickly. Unfortunately, I didn't stay that way. Thankfully, my nightmare started later than normal, so I slept longer than usual. The car accident that crushed almost every bone in my knee and resulted in the plate in my leg had left a scar that went deeper than the ones left by the surgeon. A year later, I still couldn't sleep through the night without waking up in a cold sweat. It didn't matter that the accident wasn't my fault. I was rear ended by a sixteen-year-old girl who had been texting on her phone. My car was thrown into another car. I worked for close to an hour to save the six-year-old kid. In all my years on the force, I'd seen so much death and destruction, I thought I was immune. Cops build up an outer layer of protection, like a scab, to keep the feelings inside. I'd seen things that would make most normal people lose their lunch. Yet, none of that kept me up at nights and caused me to question my vocation like the images of that kid's face, wearing one red shoe and clutching a Barbie doll. I don't know if I would ever be able to look at one of those dolls again.

Once sleep was gone, I went downstairs to my garage. I used to run when the nightmare started, but the impact was causing my good knee to ache. Instead, I went down to my garage. I created a workshop on one side of the garage that allowed me to do wood working, something I enjoyed. My townhouse was an end unit, so I didn't worry about disturbing my neighbor by using power tools at three in the morning.

I really was making a mantle for Paris' house, but I wasn't going to give it to her for her birthday. I'd found the mantle at an old salvage shop and it matched one in a picture she had of her house in the library archives from one hundred years ago. It had about fifteen layers of old paint which I sanded off. The mantle was ornately carved and once I'd sanded all that I could, I used a chemical stripper, sandpaper and old fashioned elbow grease to remove the remaining paint. I'd just about gotten it down to the natural wood and found the process of sanding by hand to be relaxing. I was able to think through the case while I rubbed the wood in mindless, rhythmic strokes.

The twists and turns in the wood reminded me of the twists and turns in this case. Samantha was not just JP Rollins daughter, she was his niece too. That was the first twist. In a town the size of St. Joe, Samantha was bound to have heard rumors from someone. Did she know her father's lawyer was responsible for killing her parents? Of course, if she did would she have wanted to kill JP or Richard Stout? Could she have found out her father was sleeping with one of her friends? Michelle doesn't seem like the type to keep a secret. If Samantha found out about the relationship, would she have wanted to keep JP from cutting her out of her inheritance? There were a lot of emotions in this case. Marie Rollins was having an affair with her husband's brother, Charles. Todd was having an affair with his wife's best friend, Natalie. And JP Rollins was fooling around with his daughter's friend, Michelle. I wondered who else was creeping around? This case was a hotbed of sex and betrayal; and had the biggest catalyst for murder, money and sex. I sanded and let the questions bounce around in my head. Right now I still had more questions than answers, but I was sure of one thing. When we got to the bottom of things, money or sex would be at the root.

CHAPTER 19

When I arrived at the precinct Tuesday morning, Harley was already there. He'd stopped by the St. Joseph Chocolate Factory and there was a large coffee and a cheese Danish on my desk. I was trying to cut back on my caffeine intake, but I loved the Chocolate Factory's coffee and their Cheese Danishes melted in your mouth.

"Thought I'd start the day off right with a ton of sugar and caffeine," he explained. "But you better eat fast or bring it with you. We just got a call. Todd Steven's plane will be touching down in about fifteen minutes."

I nodded, shoved the Danish in my mouth and took a huge swig of coffee as we headed out the door.

As we got into the car, I wondered, for the first time, where Todd planned to stay. Like a married couple, after working together for a while, Harley and I tended to read each other's minds far too often. I knew he'd read mine when I slid behind the wheel of the car because he said, "I'll bet he'll be staying with Natalie now."

Weird how spending a lot of time with someone made you think along the same lines.

"The airport will hold him, if we need them to," He added as he buckled up.

St. Joe is a relatively small Midwestern town with a population of a little over one hundred thousand. If it weren't for MAC-U, I doubted if we would have an airport, but football weekends brought a ton of visitors and business to town. The airport didn't compare with O'Hare, LaGuardia or LAX, but it was actually quite nice, given the size of the town.

We arrived at the airport in twenty minutes and were waiting near the gate outside of the luggage carousel. At sight of us, Todd looked around and then walked over to us.

"You guys the welcome wagon?" He asked.

While I hardly thought it possible, Todd Stevens looked worse than he had at the reception. Blood shot eyes, grisly faced with two day's worth of facial stubble, and he looked like he'd aged a lot in the week he'd spent on his honeymoon. I almost felt sorry for him. Almost.

"We would like to ask you a few questions." I said.

Just then the light above the carousel went on and the conveyor belt groaned and then started to roll. The masses of men, women and children hanging around between carousels migrated like lemmings to the moving belt and crowded in to grab their luggage.

"Okay if I grab my luggage?"

We nodded our consent.

Todd nudged his way closer to the conveyor belt and waited. After a while, the crowds thinned as people grabbed their luggage and made their way outside. A large duffle arrived. Todd grabbed it and hoisted it over his shoulder as he approached us.

He glanced, furtively around the airport.

I followed his glance and watched as he made contact with Natalie Jordan.

She spotted Todd and immediately rushed toward him. Perhaps she was blinded by love, but she was almost upon us before she noticed the strained look in his eyes, the barely noticeable shake of his head, or that her boyfriend was flanked by two policemen. She halted abruptly, arms midway in a hug and turned away.

"Miss Jordan, fancy meeting you here," I said.

Natalie turned back toward us. "Hello. I was just going to give Todd a lift."

"We need to have a few words with Mr. Stevens. But, you're welcome to wait."

"Look guys. I haven't had anything to eat and I'm starving. Mind if we grab something?" Todd nodded toward the small airport café just on the other side of the luggage retrieval area.

"Not at all." I nodded.

We all walked toward the café. We went inside and found a table for four away from the few other diners. Harley sat next to Todd and I sat directly opposite, leaving Natalie to sit directly opposite Harley. This allowed Harley and I to keep eyes on each of them and minimized their ability to pass any hidden signals.

The waitress, an elderly woman with a limp and a sour attitude, took Todd's order of bacon, eggs, toast and coffee. Natalie ordered a coke and Harley and I declined.

When the waitress left I looked him in the face. "We need to ask you some questions. Mr. Stevens."

The way he failed to make eye contact, told me he was afraid. The way he held his shoulders told me he was tense. The way his leg wouldn't stop jiggling told me he was nervous. The way he kept tapping his hands on the table told me he was stressed. Whether it was the memory of the discussion I'd had with my class the previous night about interrogation techniques and body language, or maybe it was just instinct, but whatever the reason, his body language was talking to me loud and clear. Here was a man who thought we had more information than we did. He was nervous and that was a good sign for us. If we played our cards right, we may be able to get him to reveal what he thought we already knew. It was worth a try.

"Why don't you tell us what really happened between you and Mr. Rollins?" I asked.

Harley took out his notebook.

"Okay, I did talk to him." His shoulders relaxed. His leg ceased jiggling and he stopped tapping his fingers. If I had to categorize his look, I'd call it relieved. He took a deep breath. "He saw Nat and me at the reception after we had…well, you know. He said he knew I was no good and I just married Sam for the money. He called us…a bunch of names." He stopped as the waitress returned with a carafe of coffee. After filling Todd's cup, she placed the carafe on the table and left Natalie's coke before leaving.

"What happened next?" I asked.

Taking a sudden interest in the patterns on the table, Todd stared at the table as if his life depended on remembering every detail. Then finally, he whispered, "Well, I tried...to threaten him."

Harley and I glanced at each other.

"Is that why you killed him?" Harley prompted.

"NO. NOT that type of threat. I *NEVER* threatened to kill him. I swear. I threatened..to tell people about him and Sam's friend. You know, I thought an important businessman like him wouldn't want anyone knowing he was screwing around with a girl young enough to be his daughter."

"You knew about JP and Michelle?"

Todd nodded, still unable to look me in the eye. "I saw the way she looked at him. I knew something was up. Then a couple of months ago, I happened to catch her sneaking out of the back of the pool house. It was dark. They didn't know I was there."

"So you threatened to expose JP Rollins affair?" Harley repeated. "How did he take that?"

Todd hung his head. "He laughed in my face. He said at his age, it would be considered a badge of honor he could still perform. Told me to call the newspapers and let him know if they wanted pictures to go with the story."

I looked over at Harley who was focused on his notepad. I doubt anyone else noticed the way his lips twitched.

"So, you tried blackmail on JP Rollins and he called your bluff. Is that when you decided to kill him instead?" I asked.

"Well, that's when I got the idea."

Harley and I exchanged glances and waited.

"I thought, he already thinks Sam is a bit of a freak. I decided to go with that. I told him Sam knew and she was already in on it."

"I don't think I understand?" Harley looked puzzled. "In on what?"

"Well, you know...me and Nat. I told him Sam knew about us and liked to watch." He hid a smirk. "I spread it on thick. I told him Sam was a freak and she liked the kinky stuff; in fact the kinkier the better. I told him a three-some was just the start. I even suggested the five of us could, well...you get the picture."

It took about fifteen second before Harley realized his mouth was open and closed it.

I was quicker. "How did JP Rollins respond?"

"I think he believed me. I mean, he just stared at me for a while, and his face got red and he looked like he was going to have a stroke. Then he called me a lot more names and told me to get out."

Seeing the look on our faces, he continued, "I swear."

"And what did you do next?" I asked.

"I left."

"So your father-in-law threatens to tell your WIFE you're cheating on her just hours after you walked down the aisle and you just left the room." I said as if talking to a first grader.

"I know it sounds crazy. But he was so drunk he just sort of fell onto the sofa." He shook his head. "I thought maybe she wouldn't believe him. He was drunk as a skunk and she knew he hated me, so, I thought if I could keep her from talking to him, maybe we could get away before he got around to her."

"What happened next?"

"I got another drink. I mean, after that, I really needed another drink. I needed time to think and I needed to find Sam to make sure she stayed away from him."

"Did you leave him in the back room on the sofa?" I asked.

Todd nodded vigorously.

"Did you see anyone else hanging around the room?"

He shook his head.

I banged my hand down on the table. "Think! Was there anyone else hanging around the room? Did anyone see you leave?" I was upset by his casual attitude, especially when it was clear he had already lied to us.

He jumped at the noise. "There were just the kitchen people. Tyler was there, looking for Kelly. I think he had just come out of the bathroom next door. He was so jealous, and he kept her on a very short leash. And, Ryan came looking for me." He shrugged. "That's it. Then, I went to find Sam."

Todd stared at me, imploring me to believe him.

After a moment, I nodded at Harley and we rose to leave.

A look of terror crossed his face and he reached out to grab me. "Please, I swear to God this is the truth. I didn't kill him."

I pulled my hand away. "When you finish your breakfast, we'll need you to come down to the station and make another statement. Don't even think about leaving town or we'll make sure it's a cold day in Hell before you see the light of day again." I turned and we walked away.

"Wait." Todd looked incredulous. "You're not going to arrest me?" He whispered so loudly people sitting nearby turned to stare.

"Not yet Mr. Stevens; but, if I find out you're lying to us, trust me when I tell you we will arrest you." I looked from Todd to Natalie. "Both of you."

I watched the blood drain from Natalie's face.

Harley and I left the airport, leaving the two lovers staring after us.

Outside, Harley asked, "Do you believe him?"

I thought about it for a few moments, before I nodded. "He's a stupid, self-centered, childish fool. But, that doesn't mean he's a killer."

CHAPTER 20

Todd arrived at the station a couple hours later and repeated everything he'd said to Harley and me at the airport. We spent another hour questioning him, before releasing him to go. We may not have gained any new insights into the murder of JP Rollins with our second interrogation at headquarters. But, we did learn more about the activities of a couple of our suspects. Turns out Frank Logan wasn't spending all of his time consoling Samantha in Reno. He'd managed to arrange to have the locks changed on the Rollins home. Todd's belongings had been placed in a storage unit; and all access to bank and credit cards had been revoked. Whether acting as a trustee of the Rollins estate, an employee of Rollins Enterprises or next in line through matrimony to inherit; Frank Logan was working to protect the assets of his former boss. In the meantime, Todd listed Natalie Jordan's address as a contact location. From the looks of things, both of the Stevens had moved on pretty quickly.

By mid afternoon, I learned Tyler Lyston had bonded out of jail. I thought about driving by to have a talk with him, perhaps I could scare him into laying off of beating his wife, at least for a while anyway. The cycle of domestic abuse meant initially, Tyler would be on his best behavior for awhile. He'd be apologetic and sorry for his behaviors. But, this wouldn't last and sooner or later, unless he got help or the wife finally got fed up and left; he would more than likely repeat the abusive behavior. The thought of seeing Tyler still made my blood boil, so I decided to delay the trip.

I got out a little earlier than usual, as Paris and I had tickets to a poetry event on campus. Probably not surprising to anyone who know me, I've never attended a poetry reading in my life. But, when Paris learned that as faculty, I was offered free tickets to the event, she was so enthusiastic; I decided it was well worth a few hours of hum drum boredom. The African American Studies Department had snagged some of the most well known African American Poets for an all day event, which would culminate tonight. I wondered what one wore to a poetry event as I dressed. My mind envisioned earthy looking people with sandals, African Kenta cloth dashikis, dread locks or beatniks with berets. Paris suggested jeans and a sweater, so I did.

She wore jeans and a white embroidered blouse that looked very crisp and clean and floated on her hips. We walked into the auditorium which was, to my great surprise, quite full. There were young, old, Black, White, and everything in between. While I saw one or two dashikis, there were probably more people in suits and ties than anything else. Thankfully, we found our seats which were in a reserved section, thanks to Judge Browning, or rather Dean Browning who snagged them for us.

Afterward, Paris and I stopped for a coffee at the St. Joseph Coffee Shop. Despite the late hour, the café was still teaming with people. We lucked out and found a small table outside on the patio just as another couple was leaving, so we were able to sit and enjoy our beverages.

The weather was beautiful and still, warm enough to sit outside. Paris was distracted, momentarily by a small dog sitting quietly beside the couple at the table next to us. She loved dogs and talked about getting one, some day. Growing up, her mom had allergies, so they weren't allowed to have a dog until Paris learned Poodles had a hyper-allergenic coat which meant most people who suffered from allergies weren't affected by the dogs. That resulted in her first dog, a small, white toy poodle named Candy. The way her eyes lit up when she spoke showed how much she loved that little dog. She was determined to get another one; but was concerned because of her crazy schedule. Eventually, the couple and Zoe, their Yorkie, left and we settled down to enjoy a peaceful break.

"How did you enjoy the poetry?" She sipped her tea and looked at me.

"I liked it a lot. It wasn't what I expected."

"You were expecting a dull, boring night weren't you?" She smiled.

"No." I lied, but at the skeptical look on her face, I laughed and admitted the truth, "okay, maybe I was."

"I know you did. That's what I like about you." She said rather coyly.

At the surprised look on my face, she explained, "I knew you didn't *really* want to go to a poetry reading. Most guys wouldn't enjoy it. But, I'm glad you were willing to go anyway. You kept your mind open to new experiences, *and* you never let me see that you didn't want to go."

I took a drink of coffee to hide my smile. "Well, I'm glad you wanted to go. It was nice. I had no idea a poetry reading could be so interesting." And I wasn't just trying to score brownie points with my girlfriend. The program consisted of readings by Harryette Mullen, Tyehimba Jess, Lana Ayers, Nikki Giovanni, and Quincy Troupe. Each had a unique style that came through as they recited, sang or told stories about their lives. Each person had a unique style. Nikki Giovanni, was a civil rights activist, professor, author and mother. She shared stories of life, equality and the highlights of events from a long and distinguished career. Quincy Troupe was probably my favorite of all the poets. Maybe I liked him most because he was a man who talked about things I could relate to, like basketball and music. Quincy Troupe was a poet, book author and performer. In between poems he talked about his incredible life and experiences with the late, Miles Davis. "I liked how rhythmic it was." I added.

"It's wonderful to hear the author reading their own words. You get their cadence and tone. There are so many different images that come to mind based on voice inflection and tone that's placed on the words." Paris added enthusiastically. "I have to admit, I wasn't a big lover of poetry when I was younger. But, I got to hear Maya Angelou read once before and after that…I was hooked."

I tried several times to discover things she might like for her birthday, but I never got a good indication of anything. Time was running out. I was almost desperate enough to ask Mama B for a suggestion, but I had a feeling that her advice would involve a ring and neither Paris nor I were ready for that; at least not yet.

When I arrived at work on Wednesday morning, Harley and I received what he referred to as a '*summons*' to Chief Mike's office. Mayor Longbow was requesting an update on the status of the case and Chief Mike wanted an update on our progress.

"This case has been going on way too long. It's cold." Chief Mike complained.

"We've had a lot of developments, especially lately." Harley added.

"Like what? Finding out JP Rollins' lawyer was a drunk and a drug addict?" Chief Mike huffed. "That's hardly what I'd call progress. Unless you can prove he killed JP Rollins? Did Rollins' discover his dirty secret and finally threaten to have him disbarred and put in jail for the murders?" Chief Mike said with only a slight twinge of hope in his voice.

Harley shook his head rather despondently.

"Harley's right. We've had a lot of developments. We've learned JP Rollins was fooling around with his daughter's friend, Michelle Hopewell. She claimed he got her pregnant. We knew he stopped seeing her about two months ago."

"Do we know why?" Chief Mike asked?

"Not yet. We also know the VP of Operations was having a fling with the boss' daughter. We know his son-in-law was sleeping with his wife's best friend and we also know JP Rollins caught them at the reception."

"But you aren't ready to arrest the son-in-law?"

I thought about that for a few moments. Todd Stevens had motive and opportunity to murder JP Rollins. He was, if not the last, then one of the last to see him alive.

"I don't like people who lie to the police." Chief Mike added, brightening to the idea of having a firm suspect. "He lied about the affair. He lied about talking to JP Rollins at the reception. Maybe he lied about killing him too." Chief Mike said.

Harley and Chief Mike looked at me for a response, but I didn't have one. Finally I added, "Maybe. I just don't think he did it. You're right, he is a liar, but that doesn't automatically mean he killed him."

"He's the strongest suspect we've got unless the girlfriend did it. What about it?"

"I can't see Natalie Jordan thrusting that knife in JP Rollins' chest."

"Maybe you two should look into the two of them a bit more. Make sure the husband didn't have a gambling problem or something."

I almost laughed out loud, "You mean make sure he didn't owe money to the mafia?" I said with barely a hint of incredulity in my voice.

"You laugh, but the mafia is everywhere." Chief Mike said. "I heard some guy on NPR talking about some book he'd just written about his life in the mob. He wasn't in a big city either. If they can get into that town, they can get into St. Joe."

I don't know what surprised me more, the fact that Chief Mike, actually believed the Mob knew where St. Joe, Indiana was, let alone that they would want to setup operations here; or the fact that he listened to National Public Radio.

"Maybe they were in it together. Maybe they planned the whole thing. This guy gets the daughter to fall in love with him. He married her, knowing he was going to kill her and get the insurance money." Chief Mike sounded excited. "I saw that on an episode of *Law and Order*."

Now *Law and Order* sounded more like the Chief Mike I knew.

"But the wife wasn't killed." Harley said.

"Maybe they didn't have time to get to her yet. Maybe that's what JP Rollins walked in on. Maybe he overheard them talking about how they were going to kill her off on the honeymoon and they had to act quickly."

"But…again, the wife wasn't killed." Harley added.

"He couldn't very well kill her after he'd just killed her father…uncle, or whatever."

Harley tried again. "I don't see how—"

"Look. I'm just throwing out ideas. If you have a better idea, by all means, let's hear it." Chief Mike paused and looked from me to Harley. After a few moments, Harley shook his head. I shrugged. And Chief Mike continued.

"I'm not saying my theories are correct, but right now, we've got nothing. All I'm suggesting is that you look a little deeper."

With that, we were dismissed. Outside, Harley whispered, "Do you think he was serious? Insurance?"

I shrugged. "I can believe that easier than I can believe Todd Stevens was a member of the mafia."

Despite our reservations about the mafia and Todd Stevens motives, we decided to delve more deeply into the backgrounds of both him and Natalie Jordan.

After a few hours, we weren't much further along. Neither Todd nor Natalie had a rap sheet. Natalie had a ton of unpaid parking tickets. She bounced a few checks but didn't have a history of it. Todd Stevens had a hard time keeping a job. In the past twenty-four months, he'd had a total of five, with none lasting more than six months. After several calls to previous employers, all off the record of course, we learned in all cases, Todd Stevens had been fired for not coming to work on time, not working while on the clock, or not coming to work at all. It was no surprise to learn Todd Stevens was lazy. None of that equated to his being a cold-blooded murderer.

I didn't have to rush to campus for class. Tonight, the class was meeting at the precinct for their ride-a-long. I was excited as the desk sergeant called to notify me there was a large contingent of students waiting in the reception area for me. I was also happy I had convinced Harley to hang around to help me get everyone situated. I think he agreed more out of curiosity than a genuine willingness to help. But, whatever his motivation, I was happy he was there.

The initial chaos of close to fifty students, some of whom were taking pictures in the precinct to send to their parents, was quickly dissipated by patrol sergeants assisting with the ride-a-long. Before long, all students were instructed on proper behavior. I verified that all consent forms were signed and accounted for, a requirement of the city attorney. If a student ended up in a violent situation, she didn't want the student or parents suing the department. Paperwork in order and all accounted for; the students were assigned to their patrol units and dispatched to prowl the streets of St. Joe.

After the last of the students left the building, Harley and I breathed a sigh of relief.

"Wow! I can't believe you have to deal with that chaos every week." Was the first thing Harley said after the students were packed off.

"Normally, it's not that chaotic. Usually, we're sitting in the class room, just talking. Today, they were pretty excited."

"You Think?" Harley's tone was sarcastic, but I could tell by the sparkle in his eyes, he had enjoyed his brief exposure to the class.

It would be easier for me to get his help in the class room the next time I asked.

Before leaving the building, we agreed on a course of action for the next day. Chief Mike was right about one thing, this case was taking a lot longer than either one of us wanted and had gotten more complicated rather than easier as the days and weeks went by. We both knew the more time elapsed, the harder it would be to catch the murderer.

It was nearly Seven thirty by the time I left the building and I decided to swing by Mama B's on my way home. I wasn't surprised to find her on her front porch rocking, with the front door open. Despite the approaching dusk, she enjoyed watching the basketball game at the recreation center across the street. Plus, her small house didn't have central air conditioning. It was autumn and the weather was cooler, but there were still days like today when the temperatures got warm.

I parked and came up on the porch. "Mama B, you know you shouldn't be sitting out here at night with the front door open like that." I kissed her cheek and then settled down in the other rocker.

I recognized several of the young men playing ball across the street from having arrested them at one time or another. It wasn't uncommon for me to come by and find about fifteen or twenty of the hardest criminals on the streets sitting on the porch drinking lemonade and eating cookies. Most people would have been scared out of their wits, but Mama B was a bird of a different feather. I was thankful she had been declared a safe zone by the local gangs. Safe didn't mean rival gangs would both meet in unity and companionship at her house. But, they were respectful of her and her property. Perhaps she reminded them of the mother or grandmother they wished they'd had. Whatever their reason, it was common knowledge on the street she wasn't to be touched.

"Too hot to sit in that house. Besides, it's a pretty good game going on." She smiled and continued to rock.

"You know what I mean."

She rocked on with a Madonna smile on her face.

We continued on in a companionable silence. Then she said, "You want some ice cream?"

I loved Mama B's ice cream. She made it from scratch, of course. It was extremely rich and quite delicious. As I rose to go into the house to get a dish of ice cream, she continued rocking. "Bring me a dish too."

We sat outside and ate homemade ice cream and watched a good basketball game, which we knew could go on well into the night. The recreation center didn't have exterior lights, but was located on a corner which was extremely well lit. For the truly intense games, the audience parked their cars around the exterior of the court and turned on their head lights. Tonight's game had been pretty intense but a last minute volley of three point shots had caused a great deal of laughter, shouts and applause from the crowd. When the crowds started to thin, I knew this game would most likely end before midnight.

"You coming to the program at the church tomorrow night?"

"What program?"

"Pastor's Anniversary." She rocked. "Paris is singing."

"I don't know. Probably. Do you want a ride?"

"I can walk."

"You know I don't like you walking through that alley at night. If I can't make it, I know Paris will pick you up and take you." I scolded, but Mama B just smiled and kept on rocking.

"You better pick me up at six-thirty then. I don't like to be late for church and that place will be packed if we don't get there early and get a seat." Mama B was a master manipulator. In one fell swoop, I knew I'd been played, but I didn't mind.

Mama B had been like a grandmother to me and my sister. Even though she wasn't actually related to our family, she'd always treated us like we were her flesh and blood. Funny but it seemed like she'd changed very little over the years, despite the fact that her hair was grayer, she walked a lot slower and she'd put on more weight than was good for her. I knew she had high blood pressure and diabetes, but talking to her about it was about as effective as talking to a brick wall. Mama B took her medicine and made a few minor modifications to her diet. She didn't add as much salt when she cooked, cut back on her pork consumption, ate a few more vegetables and drank less juice. But, she made it pretty clear to both me and her doctor that she wasn't about to give up the things she enjoyed. Her philosophy was life was too short to spend it worrying about dying. So, she intended to live each day and when the 'Good Lawd' saw fit to take her home, then He would do it; high blood pressure or not.' I tried to explain the 'Good Lawd' had given her common sense and expected her to use it to take care of her body which was the temple of God. But, we'd come to an impasse. Mama B was in her mid-sixties and hopefully had a good many years left. But, she was stubborn and regardless of what I wanted, it was ultimately her life and her decision.

I stayed a bit longer but then took our bowls into the kitchen. I washed them and put them in a rack to drain before taking my leave. I had a busy day tomorrow and now I had a busy evening too. I'd need to get some rest. I still had to swing by the station to make sure all of my students made it back in one piece. That wouldn't look good to have any of them injured during my first month of teaching. I'd left my number with the desk sergeant in the event of an emergency and thankfully, I got no calls. But, our two hour ride-a-long was scheduled to end shortly and I wanted to check back at the precinct, just in case.

I took out my keys and prepared to leave.

"Don't forget to get my Tupperware back from Harley." She rocked.

I kissed Mama B and left her as I'd found her, rocking on the porch.

Harley and I agreed to meet early for coffee Thursday morning at Adamo's Bakery. Adamo's was an Italian Deli and Bakery within walking distance of the precinct and served the best donuts on the planet. Harley was already there when I arrived and had ordered a large coffee and an Old Fashioned donut for me.

"Tell me, did all your students survive their night out on the town?" Harley shoved one of the lemon filled powdered donuts he liked in his mouth. If the powdered sugar on his chin was any indication, this was not his first one of the morning.

"Yep. All present and accounted for. If you thought they were hyped before the ride-a-long, you should have seen their faces when they got back to the station."

Harley laughed as he sipped his coffee. "Don't tell me there was a massive crime wave last night in sleepy St. Joe?"

"Thankfully not, but I think all of them had some event that kept them interested. I was a bit worried they would be bored just cruising the dark, lonely streets. But apparently, things were more exciting."

"Really? What happened?"

I wiped my sticky fingers on a napkin, and ticked off each event one by one, "One DUI high speed chase; one burglary with foot pursuit, and the mack daddy of all was a domestic violence incident that turned into a hostage situation."

Harley nearly choked on his coffee. "Are you joking? All that in one night in St. Joe? He stared. "On a weeknight? "He shook his head. "That much action doesn't usually happen in a month."

I worked to prevent a smile. Here I was worried the students would be so bored by riding along when very little happens on a normal week night in St. Joe and they had the time of their lives. I won't go so far as to say I was happy for a high crime night, but I was glad there was enough to keep the class interested. "I know. Surprised me too."

"What hostage situation? I didn't get a call?" Harley asked.

"Didn't last long enough to merit a call. The uniforms were already there for the domestic violence and the guy pulled a gun and held it to his own head, saying if his wife left, he'd kill himself."

It took a moment, but when the actual visual came into Harley's mind, he laughed. "Seriously? How drunk do you have to be to hold yourself hostage?" Harley chuckled.

I shook my head. "I have no idea. But he must have been pretty far gone. The wife put up with it for about thirty minutes while they tried to talk him down, but then she said she was tired and walked out. But get this, as she was leaving, she told him if he was going to kill himself, he'd better make sure he didn't miss 'cause she'd just got the carpets cleaned."

Harley and I both laughed at this.

"She told him if he survived and messed up her clean carpets, she'd finish him off herself."

By this time, we were both laughing so hard, people at nearby tables started laughing too.

After a few minutes, Harley wiped the tears from his eyes. "Wow! That was an exciting night."

My cell rang as we were leaving to go to the precinct.

"RJ Franklin."

"Detective Franklin, this is Henrietta Thomas. Would you be able to stop by the bank for a few moments?"

"Sure. Are you available now?" I asked, somewhat surprised to hear from Ms. Thomas, especially this early in the morning.

"Yes. That will be fine." She hung up. Our bank president wasn't one for a lot of small talk. Something had happened and I hoped this was the break we needed.

I told Harley about the call as we headed outside. First State Bank's main branch was actually only a few blocks from Adamo's, so we walked the short distance which allowed us to enjoy the lovely Autumn morning in all its glory and burn off the donuts and coffee we'd just consumed.

We arrived at the bank in less than five minutes. We saw Ms. Thomas in the lobby, talking to one of the tellers, and she waved us to her office where we waited briefly until she joined us.

"Sorry to keep you waiting." Ms. Thomas said as she hurried in and quickly moved behind her desk to her seat. Once seated, she started in at once.

"I just wanted to update you both on a situation relating to JP Rollins's estate." She sat up very straight. "I've engaged an attorney and have called a special meeting of the trustees to JP Rollins estate in light of the recent developments."

"What developments?" I asked.

"This is a highly unusual situation." She stared from Harley to me. "As you know, there are three trustees to JP Rollins estate and trust and one of them, Frank Logan is romantically involved with the beneficiary, which I believe compromises his situation. The other trustee, Richard Stout is...temporarily incapable of performing his duties." She pursed her lips. "The beneficiary of the trust is a suspect in the death of her guardian and has filed divorce from her spouse, fled to another state to establish residence." Henrietta Thomas looked flustered, something I'd never seen. It was almost comical.

"What exactly are you expecting the attorney to do?" I asked.

She held her hands open and shrugged. "I don't know. I just want to make sure everything is handled ethically. JP Rollins' estate is a large one and I feel I would be derelict in my duty if I didn't ask for guidance to ensure that decisions were made in an unbiased manner."

"Is there anything in particular that concerns you?" Harley asked.

Ms. Thomas hesitated a moment or two too long before answering. "Honestly, I don't know. I believe JP Rollins would be ecstatic that Sam is divorcing her husband. He never believed the marriage would last very long once her husband realized he wouldn't get his hands on the money." Ms. Thomas paused and took a deep breath. "But, with Richard in rehab, and Frank, cohabitating with Sam, running the company and being a trustee, it just doesn't feel right." She finished.

"What do you think should happen?" I asked.

"I think Frank Logan should step down as trustee. He is Vice President of Operations, a trustee of the estate, and in a couple of months will, apparently be married to Samantha Rollins…ah Stevens. I don't know how he can make decisions that are unbiased and in the best interest of the estate when he is personally involved."

"Good point." Harley added.

"What happens now?" I asked.

"Well, I called Frank Logan this morning and he will be flying back this afternoon to attend the meeting. I suspect he'll resign as trustee."

"Who will take his place?" I wondered.

"JP Rollins was very thorough and provided names of alternate trustees. One of the alternates will be asked to step in." She said.

"May I ask how Frank Logan took the news?" I asked?

"I think initially, he was surprised. He wanted me to wait. But, JP Rollins Enterprises is a big company. Running the company requires day to day oversight and…well, he just isn't in a position to do that right now. At least, that's my opinion."

Ms. Thomas telephone rang, and it was clear she would be leaving for another appointment. Our meeting was over.

"What time is the meeting?" I asked as we got up to leave.

"Four this afternoon in the board room here at the bank." She rose to escort us out of the office.

Harley and I discussed this new twist as we made our way back to Adamo's for our vehicles. Could Frank Logan have killed JP Rollins, thinking he would marry Samantha and then have control over the estate and the trust? It was clear we'd need to take another look at the will. JP Rollins had been concerned about protecting his money from Todd Stevens. But, would the restrictions he'd placed on Sam's spouse apply to anyone else? As a trustee, would Frank Logan have the authority to make changes which would increase his access to the money? These were perplexing questions we hadn't thought of, but thankfully Henrietta Thomas had. We decided to take a copy of the will to our own legal specialist.

CHAPTER 21

A quick call was all that was needed to let us know Judge Browning was on campus in his office this morning. A speedy walk back to Adamo's and we were in my car and heading off to MAC-U's campus.

MAC-U's campus was beautiful, especially in the autumn. The leaves were changing colors on the trees as well as on the ivy-covered buildings that looked as though they were taken right out of a painting.

Judge Browning had a large office in the Law School Building which was located near one of the two lakes the campus was built around. The building itself was made out of Indiana Limestone and covered with ivy. The interior was older, but had a great deal of charm. The halls were wide with stone walls and Terrazzo marble floors; beautiful to look at, but treacherous in the winter once they got wet from snow. We passed large lecture rooms as we made our way to Dean Browning's office. High ceilings with murals, stained glass and tons of character were everywhere we looked. The architecture was grand and the building was impressive. What the building didn't have was air conditioning in the summer, good plumbing, or adequate heating. The stained glass windows were beautiful, but drafty and the building had a stale, moldy odor that never went away.

Judge Browning's office was large with magnificent views onto the courtyard. He greeted us and we sat down across from him at his massive walnut desk and waited while he looked over the will. He was under a time constraint, so his initial reading was brief and didn't uncover any major revelations. He promised to look at the will in greater detail when he got out of his meeting with the president of the university. We left the copy of the will with him and arranged to meet him for a late lunch at two at the MAC-U Inn Restaurant.

Back at the precinct, we updated Chief Mike on the latest developments surrounding the case. The Chief was only slightly interested, especially after we weren't able to confirm his theories of mafia connections and perhaps in the light of a new day, the theories didn't seem quite so appealing.

We finished a bit of paper work and then decided to have a talk with Tyler Lyston. I'd been putting off this visit but I knew I needed to get it done sooner or later, so we headed out.

The 1963 Ford Falcon was still parked outside in virtually the same location as the last time we were there. In fact, the entire place looked pretty much the same. The toilet was still sitting in the front yard, although without Kelly Lyston, perched atop, it looked even trashier than before. Not that a woman sitting on a toilet in the front yard of her trailer is exactly classy, but taken in the context of the car on blocks, over grown grass and shabby appearance of the trailer, it didn't exactly scream 'sophistication.'

We knocked on the door and waited. Eventually, Kelly Lyston came to the door. While it didn't seem possible that her face could look worse than it had a couple days earlier; but from my days of playing sports in high school, I knew the healing process could actually look worse than the initial injury. Her face was black, blue and purple and she wore extra makeup, probably in a misguided attempt to hide some of the bruises. One glance at us and she backed up and stepped aside so that we could enter.

Inside the trailer, the shabbiness was exaggerated. The torn, tattered and badly stained, sagging sofa took up the majority of space inside the dingy living area. The large fifty-inch flat panel TV took up the remaining space. Harley and I had to turn sideways to pass by without bumping into it. The lights were out and very little light filtered through the newspapers that covered the windows, so it took a few moments for my eyes to adjust to the darkness.

Kelly Lyston sat on a tattered vinyl kitchen chair and waved her hand for us to sit.

Harley and I sat down and I didn't even pretend not to stare at her face.

"Is your husband home?" I asked more gruffly than I intended.

She shook her head. "No. He's working."

"Are you okay?" Harley asked very softly.

She nodded and sniffed, and turned her head away, hiding the full impact of the damage. "It's not as bad as it looks. I always bruised easy." She sniffed.

On the table was a large vase with a dozen long-stemmed roses. The fragrance of the flowers in the tiny confines of the trailer was overpowering. I knew from departmental training classes on domestic violence, the roses were a part of the vicious cycle of abuse. First there's the anger and rage which led to the abuse. This was followed by a period of regret. This phase was often characterized by demonstrations of affection. Women were often showered with lavish gifts and received apologies and promises never to repeat the behavior.

We sat in silence for what seemed like a long time, but was in reality probably more like a minute. There didn't seem to be a great deal to say, now that we were here.

"When will he be home?" I finally broke the silence.

"Late. One of his friends got a job doing some landscaping for some rich people on Pill Hill. He's trying to earn some extra money."

"Mrs. Lyston, you know there are places you can go. We can protect you." Harley tried, but was halted by the look in her eyes as she shook her head.

"You don't understand. He isn't bad. He really isn't. He loves me so much. He is a good man. He just has a bad temper and sometimes, I—"

I raised a hand to stop her. "Come on Harley." I stood up to go. "Look. I've heard this before." I took out a business card and dropped it on the table. "If you need help, call me. If you want to get out, we will come and help you." I then turned and walked out.

We decided not to go back to the precinct but to head back to MAC-U's campus. We were slightly early, but it was still a wonderful day and a walk around campus would be a good way to spend a few minutes.

MAC-U's campus was primarily designed for pedestrians, so parking was never easy. As a private university, MAC-U was somewhat closed off to the public. The campus was arranged so vehicles could drive around the outskirts of the beautifully manicured grounds. The buildings the public accessed were located on the outskirts. There was a major auditorium where the basketball and hockey teams played. The Athletic and Convocation Center was often booked for concerts and various theatrical performances that hit the city. I remember as a child going to the ACC to see Earth, Wind and Fire, Stevie Wonder, and the Jackson Five. As I got older, I attended both men and women's basketball games there. In fact, the women's basketball team had won a couple of national championships and was always one of the top-rated teams in the nation. In high school, I played basketball and at the end of the regular season, the area schools competed in sectional and regional games on this very court. The football stadium where Harley and I attended the season opening, was located across the street from the ACC.

MAC-U's campus had two main entries for cars. Both were gated and manned with guards that controlled vehicle traffic onto the campus. Unless your car possessed the appropriate sticker, you were halted at the gate and grilled as to where you were going, how long you would be and when you thought you might possibly be leaving. Thankfully, a police badge opened a great many doors. However, as a member of the faculty, I was given a sticker for my car which meant that I no longer had to stop and show my badge. Now, I merely slowed down enough for the guard to read the sticker on the front windshield and the gate was lifted and I was waved through. There were some nice perks to this teaching gig.

Many locals complained about the limited access to the campus. In the early seventies the campus was much more open and people were allowed to drive through at will. When a young co-ed was raped on campus, the university closed down the campus in an attempt to protect the students. The locals saw the gates as a symbol of the university's elitism. Over thirty years later, the gates stood and MAC-U's relationship with the community remained strained.

Harley and I arrived at the Inn a few minutes early and were escorted to the table Dean Browning reserved near a window that overlooked the golf course. By the time our beverages arrived, E.L. Browning spotted us and headed our way.

He had a briefcase and an arm full of files which he plopped down in one of the spare chairs. "Sorry I'm late. I was overseeing a moot court trial and the deliberations took longer than I thought."

Harley looked puzzled, "I thought you retired from the bench?"

E.L. laughed and paused while the waiter brought a cup of tea before he explained, "Oh I did. A Moot Court is a simulation. It gives the law students an opportunity to practice writing briefs, arguing their cases, the whole nine yards."

The waiter returned and we ordered our meals. Harley ordered the same French dip sandwich he'd had the last time when we were here. Judge Browning ordered a salad, stating his doctor was putting him on a strict diet. He'd been ordered to lower his cholesterol by any means necessary. I decided on the Rainbow Trout. As before, the food was delicious. By mutual consent, we didn't discuss JP Rollins will until after we'd finished our meals.

"Well, I've enjoyed the food and the fellowship, but I know you gentleman want to hear about the will." E.L. reached over to the briefcase he'd placed in the chair and pulled out the folder with JP Rollins will. Putting on his glasses, he opened the folder and looked it over briefly before closing it. "I'm sure you know the conditions of the will are very unusual. It looks like JP's primary concern was making sure his daughter and her husband didn't get control of his money."

"Why did he even bother leaving it to her at all?" Harley asked, "I mean, I've heard of people disinheriting their family.

If he was that concerned, why not leave all his money to his cat or dog or some charitable organization."

"Despite what you may see on television, that type of thing is very uncommon, especially when you're talking about someone as rich as JP Rollins. The courts would never have supported it."

"What do you mean? If it's his money, can't he leave it to whoever he wants?" Harley asked.

"Not really." E.L. leaned in to explain, "Theoretically yes, you can leave your money to whomever you want. But, relatives can always challenge it. They can tie things up in court so long that all the affected parties could be dead before a resolution is determined. The courts might determine if the daughter was living in the house, and was the sole heir, and if JP had always provided for her, she would have a right to expect he would continue to provide for her."

"What about this case? Henrietta Thomas is calling a special meeting with the trustees. What do you think?" I asked.

"I think Henrietta Thomas is a smart woman. Given the lengths JP went to in order to tie up the funds from his daughter, I think her being married to a trustee and a company officer is definitely a concern."

"What do you think will happen?" I asked.

E.L. sat back in his chair and looked out over the tops of his glasses, in the way I'd seen him do so many times before right before delivering his opinion in court. "I think if Frank Logan is going to marry Samantha, then he will probably need to step aside as trustee. There is nothing in the law that prevents a trustee from marrying the beneficiary. However, in this case, I think he would be faced with a conflict of interest and would not be able to make decisions that are objective."

We stayed on for a few moments talking but had to leave to make it to the bank in time for the meeting. Henrietta Thomas said the meeting would start at four and we needed to swing by the precinct first.

When we arrived at the precinct, there was a message from Henrietta Thomas that Frank Logan had arrived early and resigned his position as trustee. The emergency meeting was cancelled. Two of the alternate trustees had agreed to step in on a temporary basis until the courts assigned permanent replacements.

Realizing we had some extra time on our hands, we decided to use it to locate Frank Logan and have a talk with him. We hoped to catch him before he headed back to Reno.

When we couldn't get through on his cell, we decided to take a chance that he'd swing by his house. I'd love to say it was good police work, but was probably more attributable to luck than actual skill. Whatever the reason, we arrived as Frank Logan was packing.

Frank Logan's home was a cottage-style ranch home in one of the multitude of new subdivisions that were rampant around the outskirts of St. Joe. What used to be farmland when I was a kid, were now subdivisions. Most were mid-priced, vinyl clad two-story, single family homes. The developers bought acres of cheap farmland and took about two to three home plans and created a neighborhood of similar properties, varying only in color, minor embellishments or lot sizes. Woodland Cove was slightly different in that all of the homes had a similar theme. These were homes designed to resemble English country cottages. There were brick, stone and wood cottages with Tudor details and small yards that surrounded a large man-made pond with a fountain. Canadian Geese had obviously found their way to the pond and could be seen swimming in the pond or sleeping on the lawns that butted up to it.

Frank Logan didn't seem surprised to see us and opened the door to admit us with barely a nod. "I've been expecting you two. Have a seat."

The interior of Frank Logan's home, in contrast to the cottage exterior, was decorated with modern furniture. From the glass tables to the black lacquered dining chairs, massive black leather sofa, and humongous projection screen that covered an entire wall. This home was a modern bachelor pad. We took him up on the invitation to sit, and made ourselves comfortable on the leather sofa which looked large enough to hold an entire football team; and probably had.

"We wanted to ask you some questions." I started as Harley took out his notepad.

"Yeah. I figured." Frank Logan sighed.

"Why didn't you tell us?" I started, but stopped at the look on his face.

"How could I? How do you tell the police investigating the murder of my boss, I have been secretly dating his daughter, that I've been sneaking around behind his back for over a year and she dumped me and was marrying someone else? You would have locked me up before I finished talking."

Frank Logan looked like a dejected teddy bear as he watched for some type of reaction.

"You had to know we'd find out sooner or later?" I said.

"I suppose so, but, I couldn't be sure. I couldn't say that's why I didn't go to the wedding. I couldn't go and watch the woman I loved marry someone else. I just couldn't."

"So why did she dump you?" Harley asked.

Frank Logan stared out the door and watched as a goose pooped on his concrete slab patio for quite some time before answering, "I hate those geese." After another long pause, he added, "She wanted us to run away like her mom and dad."

"And you didn't want to?" I asked.

"I worked for JP Rollins for many years. I knew how vindictive he could be. I knew he'd track us down and make sure we paid for it."

"How? You're both adults. There's nothing he could legally do to either one of you." Harley stated with the calm assurance that only a police officer can have. In the books, the police protected you from bad things. The reality of life was never quite so simple.

Frank Logan stared at Harley as if he were a misguided child before adding, "I've worked for JP Rollins for over ten years. I've seen him in action. He could be mean and vindictive. He'd disinherit her." He quickly added, "of course neither one of us cared about the money. But he'd make sure no one would hire me."

"Are you sure of that? You'd worked for him for a long time. He was a football fan and over the years, you'd earned his respect." I added.

He shook his head. "I'm sure. I was good enough to work for him, but I don't think anyone was good enough for Samantha. Certainly not me."

"Well, compared to Todd Stevens, I would think you would have looked like Prince Charming." Harley added.

Frank Logan chuckled. "By that time it was too late. When I wouldn't run away with her, she dumped me and started dating Todd."

"And JP Rollins never knew that the two of you had been dating?" I asked.

Frank Logan shook his head. "Trust me, if he'd known, I wouldn't still be working for Rollins Enterprises. I certainly wouldn't have been made a trustee."

"How long ago was the break up?" Harley asked.

"About two months ago. I think she just married that jerk to make me jealous."

"Did it work?" Harley surprised us both by asking.

"Yeah. I was jealous— Of course I was. I love Sam. I've been in love with her for some time. And, now I know she loves me too." Perhaps it was the skepticism in my eyes or the smile Harley tried unsuccessfully to hide, but Frank Logan added, "No seriously. I do love her. I know we don't make any sense together. First off there's this ten year age difference. Then there's that whole Gothic thing she insists on doing. But when you really get to know her, she's funny and smart and she loves football. It's awesome."

"Are you saying that when she learned her husband was cheating, she called you?" Harley asked.

"Yeah. She was upset. She realized right away she'd made a huge mistake."

"Whose idea was it to fly to Reno?" I wondered.

"Hers actually. She saw some old movie on television about four women who were all staying on some ranch in Reno trying to establish residency so they could get quickie divorces. She asked if that was real."

"I Googled it and sure enough, you can get a divorce in six weeks in Nevada provided the other party doesn't contest the divorce. I thought it unlikely he would, especially once he knew the terms of JP's will."

"And when did *you* learn the terms of the will?" I wondered if this gentle giant could have been cold, calculating enough to have planned this whole charade. Did the two of them plan this whole crazy thing? Once they knew the terms of the will, did they arrange for Sam to marry someone JP Rollins would be vehemently opposed to, and then kill him, so Sam would be positioned to inherit the estate while her husband, the VP of Operations and trustee controlled the purse strings?

"I didn't find out JP had changed his will until afterwards. Stout called and told me."

We spent another half hour talking to Frank Logan but didn't learn anything new, except that Frank Logan believed he was the father of Samantha's baby.

CHAPTER 22

Harley and I had a little time to talk in the car on our way back to the precinct but we were probably more confused now than ever before. Michelle Hopewell was supposedly carrying JP Rollins child. Now, Samantha Rollins-Stevens-soon-to-be-Logan was pregnant too. It would be several months before either woman could prove paternity but Frank Logan seemed convinced that Samantha was carrying his child. Samantha claimed, according to Logan, she 'knew' the baby was his. And he believed her. Wonders would never cease.

Back at the station, I dropped Harley off and then hustled my butt to pick up Mama B for church service. She was sitting on the front porch, rocking as I screeched to a stop in front. She coughed and waved away the dust as she got up and walked down the stairs to get into the car. I hopped out and hurried to hold the door open for her.

Tonight Mama B was sporting an extremely bright, canary yellow hat with purple flowers. Her dress was also yellow with large splashes of purple that resembled an abstract painting. Her shoes and purse were both lavender. She was a vision.

"You're late." Was all she said.

I closed her door, went around to the driver's side and got in. I ignored the comment while I executed a U turn in the alley. "Service doesn't start for another fifteen minutes." I added as I put the car into gear. "And I can have you there in less than one minute." I joked and revved the engine.

"I would prefer to get there in one piece if you don't mind."

I was only slightly joking about the time. The church was only two blocks down the alley. I pulled up to the front of the church and stopped in the unloading zone at the curb. I hopped out and ran around to the passenger door and helped Mama B out. She climbed out of the car.

"Thankfully, I know you. So, I figured you'd be late." She smiled. "So, I told Laura Leigh to put my prayer book and a shawl on the pew and save us both seats."

I smiled and hurried around to move the car. The parking lot was jam packed and it took me longer to park the car than it had to drive from Mama B's house. I eventually found a spot at the back of the overflow lot and hurried into the church. Inside, the ushers had already started putting out chairs down the center aisle. Fire regulations prohibited chairs on the sides, but from time to time, these regulations were ignored. Tonight was one of those times. Fortunately, the sides were still pretty wide, so I knew we'd be safe.

Laura Leigh Jackson, was a forty-something southern maid with a West Georgia accent and a member of the usher board. She had saved Mama B a seat on her pew of choice, fourth from the back, and was manning her post at the door. She spotted me and smiled. Before I started dating Paris, I always felt Laura Leigh had an ulterior motive behind her smile. For all I knew, maybe she still did. She was an attractive woman, but there was a certain amount of desperation, that made me, and I suspected every other single man she met, nervous. She directed me to Mama B's favorite spot where she was waiting. She had a smug look on her face that I chose to ignore. Upon my arrival, she removed her shawl which was holding a seat near the aisle and slid over to allow room for me to sit.

The Pastor's Anniversary was a huge success with visiting churches and choirs from all over the city. Paris directed the children's choir and sang with the Gospel Chorus. Tonight she didn't lead any songs, but there were tons of excellent singers on display. All of the choirs performed well. The Drill Team, Sign Choir and even the male chorus performed. Pastor Hilton V. Hamilton, as the guest of honor, was showered with gifts and accolades all night long. He looked on with pride and several times I saw him wipe away tears as he received the appreciation of the congregation. The fundraising had been a huge success. Each auxiliary presented Pastor Hamilton with their gifts of love, one by one. Keeping a running total in my head, I calculated Rev. Hamilton was taking home close to thirty-six thousand dollars cash. He was definitely well loved and appreciated and the congregation had bent over backwards to demonstrate that love to him. The money was a huge bonus but the big surprise was that the congregation was sending Pastor Hamilton on a trip to the Holy Land. One of the other large churches in the city sponsored annual trips to Israel and we knew Pastor Hamilton had always dreamed of going. Several other members from the congregation had gone and several times Pastor Hamilton had planned to go, but something always came up at the last minute to prevent his leaving. This trip was bought and paid for and he would be leaving in just a few weeks. Ecstatic didn't begin to describe his reaction. There were very few dry eyes in the building after that final gift was presented. No one who'd contributed towards the various fundraisers could have anything except pride in knowing they had brought so much joy to someone as nice as Rev. Hamilton.

The program was a long one and lasted nearly three hours. Paris had gotten a ride to church. It would take some time before she would be able to leave and so Mama B and I sat on the porch outside of the church and fellowshipped while we waited.

Rev. Hamilton was one of the last to leave, wanting to personally thank everyone who had come and done so much for him. He stood at the door and shook hands, kissed babies and hugged everyone that came through. When Paris finally came outside, there were only a few stragglers left.

"I'm thinking you might need a police escort Reverend. It's not safe walking around with that much cash." I joked as Rev. Hamilton sat down on the porch to join us.

Rev. Hamilton laughed. "Well, considering I just have to go next door, I think I'll be fine, but I appreciate the offer."

Paris came out just as the ushers were turning out the inside lights and locking the door.

"I'm glad you'll have some spending money while you're visiting Israel. You should buy yourself something nice." Paris joked.

Rev. Hamilton smiled, pensively before adding, "I have always wanted to see the Holy Land. To walk the streets that our Lord walked, to see the place where he was crucified, and to see the tomb...ah..." He was too emotional to continue and merely shook his head at the very idea.

"I hope you have a wonderful time." Paris gave Rev. Hamilton a hug.

We rose. I had already brought the car to the curb, so the ladies wouldn't have far to walk.

"What about you?" Paris looked at Mama B. "Why don't you join the trip?" Paris joked.

Mama B smiled. "Lawd, No. Unless you can figure out a way to get me there without getting on one of them airplanes, I ain't going nowhere. I'm too old and too fat to be up in the air."

"Ah come on, Mama B" I joked. "You flew to California once didn't you?"

"Yes and I made a promise to the Lawd, if he got me back on the ground safe, I'd never go up in no more air planes again; especially now, with all them terrorist jacking planes and flying 'em into buildings. No Lawdy."

"You know they say airplanes are safer than cars." I added. "You're more likely to be in a car accident than an airplane crash."

Mama B just smiled.

"Rev. Hamilton isn't afraid, are you?" Paris added.

"*God has not given you a spirit of fear.*" Rev. Hamilton quoted as he helped Mama B into the car.

"See you can't argue with the good book." Paris quipped.

"Baby, the good book also says he will give me two wings to fly away. As soon as those wings show up, I'll be glad to use them. Until then, I'm keeping my flat feet on the ground."

We all laughed at that. In fact, I chuckled about that until I fell asleep. My mom used to say, Mama B could make a dog laugh. I think she might have been right.

Friday we learned two of the Rollins Enterprises board members, Dr. Michael Littlefield, Dean of MAC-U's business school and Dr. Jefferson Austen, former Chief of surgery at St. Joseph hospital and father of Assistant District Attorney Tim Austen, were the newest trustees for Rollins Enterprises. I wasn't familiar with Littlefield, but Jefferson Austen was well known in the community and his family's philanthropy was legendary in St. Joe. Jefferson Austen was revered for making annual trips to war torn, third world countries where he donated medical supplies as well as his time and expertise to help the poor and disadvantaged. This liberal humanitarian seemed an unlikely associate of JP Rollins. Two more diverse people were hard to imagine. Dr. Jefferson Austen and JP Rollins must have been very interesting in a board meeting together.

This case was getting to me. It had been two week and we weren't any closer to figuring out who killed JP Rollins. I knew we were missing something, but for the life of me, I didn't know what it was.

I arranged to take a half day of vacation. In the past, I worked seven days per week, almost 365 days per year. But a few months ago, Human Resources, and the policemen's union decided to enforce the vacation policy and I was forced to take time off. Don't get me wrong. I liked vacations as much as the next guy. However, I couldn't help noticing whenever you took time off, the work continued to come in. Coming back from vacation with work piled up made me more stressed than just not taking the time off to begin with. However, I turned over a new leaf. Well, maybe turned over is an exaggeration. At least, I've lifted the leaf and rotated it around. At least, a half day of vacation here and there was a start. In the meantime, I tried to get as much done in the morning as possible. Harley and I spent the morning going through the statements and created a timeline, mapping out our key suspects minute by minute. Tedious and time consuming, but it helped. If you took a specific point in time and checked where each person said they were and then took the next point and checked statements and verified movements. It could often be helpful. Unfortunately, nothing immediately leapt out at us. But there was something. I just couldn't put my finger on it. Like a feather blowing in the wind, the missing point floated around and around, never landing within reach, but floated just outside of the edge of consciousness. Experience told me to stop trying to grab at it. So, I did. It was lunchtime and I had a date.

Thirty minutes later I was seated at a table at the Cracker Barrel with a newly coiffed Mama B. Paris generally did Mama B's hair on Fridays to prevent the long waits she had on Saturdays. Plus, Mama B liked to have her hair *'fresh'* when she went to the Missionary Society Meeting which was later in the afternoon. Mama B kept her hair just long enough to allow Paris to roller set. I had learned far more about women's hair than I ever dreamed since I started dating a stylist. I honestly couldn't tell the difference between a roller set and any other type of set; but I was too smart to admit that to either Mama B or Paris.

Normally, Mama B wasn't a fan of restaurant fare, with the exception of the Cracker Barrel and Red Lobster. The Cracker Barrel was a chain that originated in the South and served good, old fashioned food with a southern flare. Mama B attributed it to a cook who knew soul food, but I doubted that was the secret to their success, but again, I wasn't going to tell her that. Whoever cooked the food, it was always well seasoned and tasty.

Mama B ordered the baked chicken and dressing with fried okra and sweet potato casserole. I went for the fried catfish with fries and coleslaw. We both enjoyed the corn bread muffins our waitress brought out for us to nibble on while we waited for our food with sweet tea. This was good stuff.

"Too bad Paris couldn't get away to join us. That girl works too much." Mama B said.

"Fridays and Saturdays are always busy times for her." I said even though I knew perfectly well Mama B already knew this.

"I'm sure you would prefer to be out with her than with an old woman like me." Mama B laughed.

"What old woman" I looked around.

"Psshaw" Mama B chuckled. "Boy you ain't fooling me. We both know I'm old as dirt."

"You're as young as you feel." I told her.

"In that case, I'm older than dirt." Mama B laughed.

We stopped as the waitress brought out our meals and asked if we needed anything else. After taking our requests for hot sauce, chutney, and extra cornbread muffins, she was off. By the time she returned, we were digging into our meals. After about ten minute of nonstop eating, I was ready to come up for air.

"That was almost as good as your cooking." I wiped my finger with the wet nap the waitress had provided.

Mama B shook her head. "You ain't fooling me. I'm just a self taught cook. I ain't got no restaurant."

"No, but you know you can throw down with the best chefs any day of the week. I'd put your Carmel Cake against anyone of those high class chefs on television in a heartbeat." I said truthfully, and meant every word.

Mama B smiled and shook her head. "Boy you know you need to stop lying before your nose starts growing."

This was our normal banter and as comfortable as an old pair of jeans and my favorite sweater.

"How's your job?" Mama B asked as we sipped coffee.

I don't know if it was the momentary hesitation before I answered or whether she really was psychic, like Harley claimed, but she added, "Seems like you got something worrying at you."

"I'm just thinking about the JP Rollins murder. I don't feel like we're making progress -seems like there's some piece missing to this puzzle."

"Well, I don't know nothing about no murder. But, I do know about puzzles. You can't put no puzzle together if you ain't got all the pieces. You just need to lay everything out and then turn the pieces right side up, so you can make out the real picture. Then sort them." She motioned with her hands as she spoke.

"What do you mean, sort them?"

"You put all the colors together. That will help you figure out what's missing." She added.

I sat there looking at her for close to a full minute before speaking. "But we've been sorting all of the evidence and, it just seems like something is still missing. I can't quite put my finger on it. We've created a timeline and cross checked all of the statements."

Mama B just shook her head.

"What?" I questioned.

"Baby, I think you're making this more complicated than it needs to be."

I shook my head. "Not necessarily. There are lots of reasons people kill and one of them is money and JP Rollins had a lot of it.

She shrugged. "People kill for money, but he been rich for a long time and nobody ain't never killed him." She shook her head. "Naw, that wasn't no money killing."

"What do you mean?" I asked.

"It took a lot of anger for somebody to take a knife and stab that man like they did."

"Why do you say that?" I stared at her. I was an experienced cop, but she was experienced with life and right now, that might be what I needed, someone with life experience. "JP Rollins was a billionaire. Money can be a big motivator for murder."

Mama B shook her head, "People will kill now a days for a dollar-fifty. But, they don't do it at a wedding with lots of people around. Whoever killed that man got up close and personal. They looked him in the eye and..." Mama B shook as if a sudden chill had gone over her. "My grandmother used to say someone was walking over your grave when you got a chill like that." She said.

The mood had gotten a lot darker. I didn't want to think about Mama B's grave, and murder was hardly the appropriate conversation for lunch. But, Mama B had given me some food for thought.

Sometimes I feel like a motherless child

Sometimes I feel like a motherless child

Sometimes I feel like a motherless child

A long ways from home

There's praying everywhere

CHAPTER 23

Most people don't like working on Saturdays, preferring instead to spend quality time with family. I actually didn't mind working Saturdays. The precinct was a little quieter, at least in the daytime. And I found it easier to think. The dress code was somewhat relaxed on the weekends. Harley and I were in jeans, as opposed to our normal, business casual attire that the St. Joe Police Department required. Based on the television shows, it appeared St. Joe was in a time warp. Somewhere between custom made suits and Levi's and t-shirts, St. Joe drew its line. It required its plain clothes detectives to maintain a level of professionalism, especially when the mayor could walk through the office at any time. Weekends were another story. Unless you had a press conference or some important meeting, you were free to wear whatever you wanted; as long as it maintained the dignity and respect of the department.

Harley and I were back at our timeline. Something was still not quite right but I still hadn't put my finger on it.

"We've looked at this timeline so many times; I think I can recite it by heart." Harley groaned.

"I just can't figure out what's bothering me."

"Hey, did you ever figure out what you're getting Paris for her birthday?"

"Not yet."

"Well, it's coming up pretty soon isn't it? It's the 30th right? Like tomorrow." Harley stretched and propped his feet on the desk.

"Thanks for reminding me."

"Anytime, that's what partners are for." he grinned and ignored my sarcasm.

"Look, how about focusing your energy on the case. Mama B said something yesterday that got me thinking."

"What did the Oracle have to say about JP Rollins?" Harley laughed. Harley had always called Mama B the Oracle, ever since he met her.

"It's not exactly what she said so much as the impression. Oh, and she wants her Tupperware back."

Harley scowled. Clearly he'd forgotten to bring it. "What did she say?"

I paced. "She said whoever killed JP Rollins must have been really angry."

"Well, duh...I mean they plunged a knife in his chest." Harley said.

"Right. It got me thinking. I mean, maybe we've been looking at this from the wrong angle."

"'splain Lucy." Harley joked in his lame rendition of a Ricky Ricardo accent.

"Normally, when a rich, powerful person like JP Rollins is murdered, you'd expect it had something to do with the money. But, maybe we haven't sorted the puzzle pieces out properly. Maybe it's not about who benefits financially from the murder."

Harley frowned. "Then why kill him?"

I stared at the timeline that was up on the whiteboard and all of the statements that were strewn all over the desks and wondered the same thing.

"I don't know. But I don't think this murder was about the money. I think it was a crime of passion. Whoever killed JP Rollins must have hated his guts."

"Well, that certainly narrows things down to about two-thirds of the population and darn near everyone that JP Rollins ever came into contact with," Harley said.

"Right. But, only a small percentage of those people would have been at the wedding."

"Good point." Harley sat up and glanced through the statements again.

I paced. "Given the statements of the wedding party and the caterers, very few of the actual guests made their way to the back. We've already eliminated the kitchen workers. I think that holds."

"Agreed. Who does that leave us with?"

"The wedding party seems the best bet. At least it's a good place to start."

Harley sorted through the statements and pulled out those of the wedding party. As Mama B suggested, we sorted the statements like pieces of a puzzle. "Ok, let's start with the women." I suggested.

"Why the women?" Harley questioned. "It doesn't fit. I know women could kill just like a man."

"True, but, this just seems like a man." I couldn't explain it. "Let's try to eliminate the people we can."

"Natalie Jordan was having an affair with the groom. JP Rollins discovered them." Harley moved to the whiteboard to look at the timeline. "She left the back room and went back out into the main reception area."

I leafed through statements, and pulled one from Michelle Hopewell, that seemed to line up the times. "Lines up with Michelle Hopewell's statement." I added. "Doesn't seem that getting caught with the groom in a compromising position would have driven Natalie Jordan to kill. I mean, she was a stripper. She's probably used to…compromising positions."

"I believe the politically correct term was exotic dancer." Harley joked.

"Whatever. What about Michelle Hopewell. She was having a fling with JP Rollins."

"She might have done it. She claims JP Rollins didn't know about the baby. What if he did know and didn't want anything to do with her. Maybe they got into an argument at the reception." Harley speculated.

"Maybe."

"You know what they say, 'Hell hath no fury like a woman scorned'. She admitted JP Rollins had cooled off on the relationship. Maybe she wasn't ready for things to end. Here she was pregnant and alone. She might have caught JP Rollins with someone else." Harley said with an enthusiasm that told me he liked this theory.

"It's possible." I hedged.

"You don't like it."

"She doesn't strike me as the type. I know…I know there's no one type of murderer. Anyone can be driven to do things that are outside of their character. It's a possibility." I admitted reluctantly.

"Next up was Kelly Lyston. What kind of passion would JP Rollins elicit in her? Harley quipped.

Something clicked in my head and I paced more rapidly.

"What? You've thought of something. You think Kelly Lyston did it?" Harley asked a bit incredulous.

"Kelly Lyston. No. I can't see JP Rollins stirring passion in Kelly. But Kelly could definitely stir Tyler Lyston's passion."

"Yeah. I can see that." Harley admitted.

The thing I'd been struggling to grasp, the idea that had eluded me for two days, finally began to take shape. I rustled through the statements until I found the one I was looking for. Harley came over to read over my shoulder.

"What is it?" He asked, "That's not Tyler Lyston's statement. That's Todd Stevens."

"Yeah. I just remembered something Todd said in his statement." I found the passage I wanted and handed the statement to Harley.

Harley was always a quick study. By the time I got my weapon, he grabbed his keys and hurried down the hall after me. One stop at the desk to request backup and we were out to get our killer.

CHAPTER 24

By the time we arrived at the trailer park, five other black and whites were pulling up with lights and sirens flashing. Harley and I had donned our bullet proof vests before leaving the precinct and as we setup a perimeter around the trailer, I realized how dangerous the situation was.

The exterior looked pretty much the same as the last time we saw it. The car and the toilet hadn't moved out of the front yard. The front door to the trailer was open and as I moved behind a protective barrier, I noticed the curtain move. Someone was home. I hoped it wasn't Kelly. This situation could very easily turn into a hostage situation, or worse, a murder-suicide.

"Tyler Lyston. This is the police. Come out of the house with your hands on top of your head." I hated using a bull horn, but hopefully the neighbors would have enough sense to stay in their homes and help minimize the risk of any innocent people getting hurt. We weren't even sure Tyler Lyston was in the house until we heard Kelly scream, the sound of breaking glass and the boom of the rifle Tyler shot out of the window. We crouched down further behind our barriers.

This was not good. Our suspect was home. He was armed and apparently dangerous, considering he'd just shot at us. Plus, he had a hostage. The SWAT Team arrived and got into position.

"Tyler. Don't make this worse than it already is. Let Kelly go."

Tyler Lyston's response was another blast from his rifle.

"Guess we take that as a NO." Harley quipped.

We were in a hostage situation. Our assailant was armed. He'd already killed once and I had no reason to believe he wouldn't do it again. I pulled out my cell.

"This isn't working." I said as I handed the bull horn to Harley. Hitting speed dial for dispatch, I told the operator we were in a hostage situation and to patch me through to the Lyston's. A few moments later, the phone rang. After about the tenth ring, it didn't seem Tyler was going to answer. That's when Harley yelled through the bull horn, "Pick up the phone." Surprised, I looked at Harley who shrugged and said, "it was worth a try."

I was actually surprised when I heard "What?" on the other end of the phone.

"Tyler this is Detective Franklin. We need to talk."

"Okay. Talk."

"A bit awkward wouldn't you say? This would be a lot better face to face. Why don't you come out?"

"Yeah–right, so you can gun me down. I'm not dumb."

"You're right. You're too smart not to see where this is going. None of us wants to have another fatality on our hands. We just need to sit down and talk. How about it?"

"Fine. You come in *ALONE* and *UNARMED*." Were the last words I heard before the phone was slammed down.

I didn't realize I'd been holding my breath until I exhaled. Harley and I exchanged glances as I handed him my weapon.

"You sure about this?" Harley asked.

"I'm sure. All I have to do is try not make him angry."

"And keep him away from the knives" Harley added with a forced grin. Seriously, "be careful."

I nodded and then, put my hands in the air. I stood slowly and waited a second, so he could see it was me. Then, encouraged by the fact that no shots had been fired, I walked toward the front door. To keep my mind occupied, I took note of the SWAT team positions surrounding the trailer. This was a heck of a situation. Statics said hostage situations rarely ended well. I was hoping this would be the exception and I continued walking toward the front door of the trailer.

CHAPTER 25

At the front door, Tyler yelled, "Step in and STOP right there."

Inside the door I stopped. My first sight was Kelly Lyston whose face was battered and bruised and streaked with tears and mascara. But the frightening sight was the shear horror I saw in her eyes. The situation was definitely terrifying, but I'm sure the rifle Tyler had to her head was a major cause for concern.

"Hold it right there." Tyler yelled. And I halted.

"Check him." Tyler ordered, using the rifle to shove Kelly towards me.

Kelly whimpered as she reached toward me and gingerly patted me down. I don't think it was lack of experience frisking for weapons, which caused Kelly to miss the backup weapon stashed in the small of my back.

It took less than a minute to assess the situation which wasn't good. I needed to try and convince Tyler to release Kelly and take me as his hostage instead. I also needed to keep Tyler focused on me, so he wouldn't notice the armed gunmen trying to get a clear shot at him in the event that things stopped being friendly.

"Okay you're here. Now what?" Tyler asked. He was, not surprisingly, jumpy and agitated as he kept his gaze on me, his gun on Kelly and his head out of the line of fire of the window.

"Tyler. I'm here to help you."

"Really? You want to help me? Then call off those snipers. Let me get out of here. That's how you can help me." Tyler yelled.

"You know I can't do that Tyler. This isn't television and that's not how this is going down."

"Right. Then how exactly are you going to help me?"

"Let Kelly go. Releasing a hostage will go a long way toward reducing your sentence."

Tyler laughed. "Hostage? She's not a hostage. She's my wife."

"That's right. She is your wife. So, you certainly don't want her to get hurt. Let her go. You don't need her. You've got me. I'll stay. They aren't going to do anything with me in here." I tried to sound confident.

I could see Tyler's hands shaking as he processed this. "I don't know."

"Yes, you do. You know what you need to do. Let Kelly go and then you and I will sit here and figure out how to get you out of this."

Kelly was shaking so badly now she could barely stand. She was close to collapse and Tyler Lyston was on the verge of a breakdown. The next few seconds were critical. If something was going to happen, I knew it would happen in the next few minutes. That's when the scales tipped.

Tyler wiped a bead of sweat from his forehead. For an instant, he relaxed his grip on the rifle, and looked over his shoulder. With a brief nod, Kelly dropped to the floor and I lunged at Tyler, one hand reached for the rifle and the other reached for my gun. The rifle blasted a hole in the wall of the trailer, just as I landed on top of him and the SWAT team swarmed into the trailer.

CHAPTER 26

Two minutes later, Tyler Lyston was cuffed and sitting on the ground, while Kelly Lyston was examined by EMTs. The SWAT Team made sure the trailer was secure and there were no other gunmen lurking around the corner just waiting to fire. When they finished, they gave the all clear.

Not surprisingly, Kelly looked scared out of her mind. She shook like a leaf.

"You OK I asked?"

Her teeth were chattering so much, she could barely talk, "Yeah…Yes." She managed to eke out. The EMT was just about to insert an I.V. When Kelly retracted her arm. "Wait…wha… what's that?"

"It's just a very mild sedative, something to help you relax. We're going to take you to the hospital and run some tests." That' about as far as he got.

Kelly furiously began to shake her head. "I ca…can't… ba…ba.. baby."

"You're pregnant?" the EMT asked; and Kelly nodded.

Harley looked down at Tyler who was propped against the wall. Then, yelled "Did you know she was pregnant? What kind of scum bag are you? You could have killed your wife and your child."

Tyler Lyston laughed hysterically, and then lunged for Kelly. She screamed, but Harley grabbed the still cuffed Tyler while I got between Kelly and Tyler just to be safe.

Tyler Lyston had a very colorful vocabulary. After spitting out a series of expletives that would have made a sailor blush, he laid down on the floor and wept like a baby.

Setting aside most of the four letter words, I figured out the motive for JP Rollins murder.

Turning to Kelly Lyston I asked, "Is that right? Is JP Rollins the father of your baby?"

"NO! NO! NO! I told him he wasn't." Kelly cried.

"LIAR! I Heard them." Tyler spat out.

"Heard who?" I asked Tyler. What did you hear?"

Sniffling, Tyler snarled, "LIAR. I was in the bathroom. I heard Todd tell him. He knew. My cousin knew you were screwing around with that old man."

"I don't know what Todd said, but I NEVER…"

"SHUT UP!"

"Hold it." I interrupted. "You overheard Todd talking to JP Rollins. Right?"

Tyler snarled, "Yes."

"And he said KELLY was sleeping with JP Rollins? Did Todd specifically say Kelly's name?"

Tyler hesitated. "He said he knew he was sleeping with Sam's best friend. And Kelly was Sam's best friend. I knew who he was talking about. I KNEW it was her." Tyler screamed and then fell over crying.

"Todd didn't know Samantha well enough to know WHO her best friend was. JP Rollins was sleeping with Michelle Hopewell. NOT Kelly." I spat the words out, disgusted at the waste of life. "So, you killed an innocent man. You killed JP Rollins for no reason."

"WHAT?" Tyler hiccupped as the reality of my words finally sunk in. "Are you sure?"

"Positive. Michelle Hopewell has admitted she and JP Rollins were having a relationship." Harley said as he hoisted a dazed Tyler Lyston to his feet. "So, you basically destroyed your life and almost destroyed the lives of your wife and unborn child."

Tyler lunged towards Kelly. "Kelly, baby, I'm so sorry. Kelly. I'm so sorry. Baby you have to believe me. I never meant to hurt you. I…"

"Get him out of here." I ordered, disgusted.

CHAPTER 27

It took hours to get all of the paperwork tied up. Thankfully, we didn't have to spend a lot of time interrogating Tyler Lyston. Once we were back at the station, he waived all of his rights to legal consul and sang like a parakeet. I had no doubt a good lawyer would be able to convince a jury Tyler Lyston was mentally unbalanced. His jealous rages had finally taken a toll on his mind rather than his wife's face. He needed help and he'd be sure to get it where he was going.

After the paperwork, we spent hours briefing Chief Mike, the mayor, the District Attorney and what felt like half the police force, but was probably just a third of them. When we finally got the okay to go home, I saw Kelly Lyston waiting in the hallway.

"Should you be here? I thought they were keeping you overnight at the hospital?" I escorted her to a seat in waiting area.

"I'm fine. And the baby is fine and that's all I needed to know. But, how is Tyler? Is he okay?"

I shouldn't have been surprised. Abused women often return to their abuser.

"He's not. But, he will be." I reassured her. "He's sick. He needs help. And, so do you." Reaching into my wallet, I pulled out a card I've been carrying around since I saw her the last time he beat her up. "Jamie's House is a treatment center run by some friends of mine. Call them."

Kelly took the card.

I doubted if she would call, but I hoped she would. Regardless, the ball was in her court now.

I was right on time for early morning service. I shocked the heck out of Mama B when I arrived at her house just as she was starting to walk the two blocks down the alley to the church. I pulled up beside Mama B, rolled the window down and hollered, "Hey good looking. How about a ride?"

I thought she would never stop laughing. Even when we were seated in our usual spot, I could tell by the way the fruit on the top of her hat shook that she was still chuckling, despite the program she used to fan and unsuccessfully tried to hide her mouth.

It was the fourth Sunday. The Fourth Sunday was generally a pretty quick service. I think the Spirituals and Anthems that were sung by the Inspirational Chorus must be shorter than the modern gospel music sung on most other Sundays. However, we were still auditioning the new Choir Directors, so today was a bit different. Today's candidate was able to showcase his versatility by directing the choir as they sang a cappella, played the piano for a rousing spiritual and played the organ for a rather stirring anthem. And the cherry on the top was a duet he sang with his wife while one of his children played the piano. Pretty impressive.

The sermon today was a message of encouragement. I left with my heart full of the knowledge of God's eternal love and a warm fuzzy feeling inside. Later, as I lounged on Mama B's porch with visions of candied sweet potatoes, cabbage, and fried chicken in my head, I was pretty satisfied. Today was August 30th and Paris' birthday. I knew there was a chocolate cake in the kitchen and homemade ice cream waiting for us. This was definitely a good day.

As the congregation started to arrive on Mama B's porch, Paris and I made our exit, Tupperware in hand. Today's walk along the East Race was extremely beautiful. The weather was perfect, neither too hot nor too cold. Hand in hand, Paris and I strolled along the river.

"You seem... different." Paris mentioned.

"Really? Different how?"

"I don't know, very satisfied." She glanced at me.

"Well, maybe I am. I just solved a murder. I'm walking with one of the most beautiful women in the world. It's a fantastic day. I guess I'm just a happy man."

Paris smiled at me and we kissed. Just when things were starting to get interesting, I felt a push.

"What the…" I turned to look, just as a black standard poodle puppy leaped in the air and tried to lick my nose.

"Ah…how cute." Paris cooed as she bent down and petted and cuddled, the puppy. "You are just the most adorable… girl" Paris said, then took a moment to check underneath and verified the gender.

"What a beautiful girl. But where's your owner." She looked around.

Standing by a nearby tree, was woman with a backpack.

"You have a beautiful dog." Paris yelled as the woman approached.

"No. Not really." She added.

Paris looked up surprised, "What?"

"She's not my dog." The woman clarified.

"Oh. Whose dog is she?" Paris looked around.

"Yours," I said, hopefully, doubting my gift for the first time. "That is if you want her."

"OH. Are you serious?" Paris face reflected first shock and then joy.

"Happy Birthday." I nudged the puppy out of the way, so I could kiss her. "Do you want her?"

"Of course I want her. She's beautiful." Paris gushed. "But are you serious? You really got her for me?"

"I did. I know you love poodles. I remember you telling me about Candy. So, I did some research. And that's when I found Marti." I turned to the woman who had been standing nearby. "Paris, let me introduce you to Marti Alexander. Marti is a breeder. She also trains, grooms, and boards dogs; and happens to be our coroner's niece."

Paris and Marti shook hands while I continued. "Marti also works with the police performing search and rescue."

"Very pleased to meet you."

"Detective Franklin tells me you lead a pretty busy life. So, I have a plan that will help you train her and make sure she's socialized, exercised and happy."

"She's beautiful." Paris gushed.

"She is indeed. She's AKC, CKC, and UKC registered. Her parents were both champion show dogs and if you decide to show her, let me know."

"She is the most beautiful dog I've ever seen." Paris mumbled as she rubbed her face against the dog's coat.

Paris beamed as she cuddled her newest love. If I weren't so confident, I might have been just the slightest bit jealous.

SOMETIMES I FEEL LIKE A MOTHERLESS CHILD

Sometimes I feel like a motherless child

Sometimes I feel like a motherless child

Sometimes I feel like a motherless child

A long ways from home

A long ways from home

True believer

A long ways from home

Along ways from home

Sometimes I feel like I'm almos' gone

Sometimes I feel like I'm almos' gone

Sometimes I feel like I'm almos' gone

Way up in de heab'nly land

Way up in de heab'nly land

True believer

Way up in de heab'nly land

Way up in de heab'nly land

Sometimes I feel like a motherless child

Sometimes I feel like a motherless child

Sometimes I feel like a motherless child

A long ways from home

There's praying everywhere

Mama B's Recipes

Crock Pot Ham

1 Ham (size for your crock pot)
1 box brown sugar
20 oz bottle coke
1/2 can frozen orange juice
1 can sliced pineapples

1. Put the ham in the crock pot. Pour brown sugar, coke, orange juice and pineapples into the crock pot and mix.
2. Cook on low for 8-10 hours or 4-6 hours on high until done.

NOTE: I rarely defrost my ham before putting in the crock pot. Thankfully, I've never cracked the crock. However, you should always follow the rules for your specific crock pot.

Depending on the size of the ham, you may want to add less of the orange juice concentrate or the glaze will be too orangey.

Elvira's Potatoes and Green Beans

6-8 potatoes
1 ½ lbs of fresh green beans
2 ham hocks
2 medium onion
Salt and Pepper
¼ cup bacon grease (optional)

1. Wash green beans and cut off ends. Cut and quarter onion and put green beans, onion and ham hocks in a 5 quart pan with water, and add bacon grease.
2. Cook over medium heat until beans are almost done, approximately 1 hour (less time if using canned beans)
3. Wash, peel, and quarter 6-8 white potatoes. Salt and pepper potatoes well before adding to green beans. Cook until potatoes are done, approximately 30 minutes.

You can substitute beef neck bone for ham hocks and extra virgin olive oil for bacon grease.

Quick and Easy Lemon Meringue Pie

8 inch graham cracker pie crust
½ cup lemon juice
1 can eagle brand condensed milk
1 Teaspoon grated lemon rind
3 eggs separated
1/3 cup sugar
¼ teaspoon cream of tartar
½ teaspoon vanilla

1. Preheat oven to 350 degrees.
2. In mixing bowl, combine EAGLE BRAND® milk, lemon juice, lemon rind, and egg yolks; stir until mixture thickens.
3. Pour into pie crusts. Put in the oven and warm while you make the meringue.
4. Add cream of tartar and vanilla to egg whites; beat until almost stiff enough to hold a peak.
5. Add sugar gradually, beating until stiff and glossy but not dry.
6. Remove pie from oven and pile the meringue onto the pie filling.
7. Bake 350 degrees F. until meringue is lightly browned (approximately 15 minutes). Cool.

Pound Cake

2 Cups (4 sticks) butter, plus more for the pans
3 Cups sugar
8 eggs
3 1/2 Cups flour, plus more for the pans
1 Cup heavy cream or milk
2 Tablespoons pure vanilla extract

1. Heat oven to 350 degrees. Grease and flour 2 loaf pans.
2. In a large mixing bowl cream together the butter, vanilla and sugar until light and fluffy. Beat in the eggs one at a time.
3. Beat in the flour alternately with the heavy cream or milk. Mix until just incorporated.
4. Pour into loaf pans and bake approximately 1 – 1 ½ hours or until a tooth pick inserted in the center comes out clean.
5. Using a knife, loosen the cake from the sides of the pan and allow to cool for 10 minutes. Remove cake from the pans and cool completely before serving.

NOTE: You can add other flavoring (eg. orange, almond or lemon) to the cake for a twist.

Smothered Chicken

1 lb chicken cut into pieces
¼ cup vegetable oil
1 Teaspoon Lawry's Season Salt
1 Teaspoon Pepper
¾ cup Flour plus 2 Tablespoons
1 medium chopped onion
1/8 cup Worcestershire Sauce
½ Cup Water
½ package Lipton Onion Soup Mix

1. Heat the oil in a large skillet on medium heat.
2. Wash the chicken well (my mom always removes the skin but I buy skinless pieces – You can leave the skin on if you prefer), and pat dry with a paper towel.
3. Season the chicken with the Lawry's Season Salt and pepper and dredge with flour.
4. Place chicken into the hot oil and cook until golden brown on all sides and then remove the chicken from the skillet.
5. Add remaining flour, onions, Worcester sauce, water, and onion soup mix to the skillet. Cook flour until brown, stirring constantly.
6. Add chicken. Turn heat to simmer.
7. Cover and cook for approximately 20 -25 minutes until chicken is soft and tender and gravy is thick.

(My mom doesn't add the Worcester sauce or Onion Soup mix but I have not yet mastered the art of making gravy without it.)

About the Author

V. M. Burns was born and raised in Northwestern Indiana where she grew up in a Baptist church very similar to the one in her novel. She also sang in the church's choir and various other choirs (similar to the ones in her novels). She holds a Bachelor's degree from Northwestern University and a Master of Science in Administration from the University of Notre Dame and a Masters of Fine Arts from Seton Hill University in Gtreensburg, Pennsylvania. She now lives in Eastern Tennessee with her two poodles.

CPSIA information can be obtained
at www.ICGtesting.com
Printed in the USA
JSHW032032150323
39008JS00005B/171